G R JORDAN

A Common Man

Inferno Trilogy 2

First edition

ISBN: 978-1-915562-23-4

This book was professionally typeset on Reedsy.
Find out more at reedsy.com

Being like everybody is the same as being nobody.

ROD SERLING

Contents

Foreword

The events of this book, while based on known areas in Scotland, are in an entirely fictional setting and all persons are entirely fictitious.

Acknowledgement

To Ken, Jessica, Jean, Colin, John and Rosemary for your work in bringing this novel to completion, your time and effort is deeply appreciated.

Novels by G R Jordan

The Highlands and Islands Detective series (Crime)

1. Water's Edge
2. The Bothy
3. The Horror Weekend
4. The Small Ferry
5. Dead at Third Man
6. The Pirate Club
7. A Personal Agenda
8. A Just Punishment
9. The Numerous Deaths of Santa Claus
10. Our Gated Community
11. The Satchel
12. Culhwch Alpha
13. Fair Market Value
14. The Coach Bomber
15. The Culling at Singing Sands
16. Where Justice Fails
17. The Cortado Club
18. Cleared to Die
19. Man Overboard!
20. Antisocial Behaviour
21. Rogues' Gallery
22. The Death of Macleod - Inferno Book 1

Austerley & Kirkgordon Series (Fantasy)

1. Crescendo!
2. The Darkness at Dillingham
3. Dagon's Revenge
4. Ship of Doom

Supernatural and Elder Threat Assessment Agency (SETAA) Series (Fantasy)

1. Scarlett O'Meara: Beastmaster

Island Adventures Series (Cosy Fantasy Adventure)

1. Surface Tensions

Dark Wen Series (Horror Fantasy)

1. The Blasphemous Welcome
2. The Demon's Chalice

Chapter 1

Macleod looked along the lonely street, now in late afternoon, and he saw very few shoppers. He wondered, as the light began to fade, how soon would it be before the street lights came on. *It is a pretty enough village*, he thought. Winston Arnold had chosen well when sourcing a location for his bookshop, albeit that the bookshop itself was of a rather strange nature. Occultic books, weird books, a shop that sold the kind of reading material you'd have to seek out. Not for Winston Arnold, the crime novels that Macleod detested, possibly in the way that anyone didn't like others from outside their trade talking about their job. Macleod couldn't watch crime on TV either. He got enough of the real thing when he was at work. Why on earth would he want to watch any more of it?

He heard a slight pitter-patter on the roof of the car and looked up at the rather delicate, in his opinion, cover. His feet were hemmed in. He felt like his shoulders didn't quite get the support from the chair behind him that they deserved, but he wasn't complaining because he no longer had the large car provided for him by the service. Macleod had been suspended from the case. Well, at least, removed from the investigation, one that according to his superior, he had made a bodge of.

Ian Lamb was the target. Ian Lamb was the man who had killed them all, and Ian Lamb was the man who was found dead in a police cell after committing suicide. It hadn't washed with Macleod. Ian Lamb, as much of a pervert as he was, was no killer. Macleod had seen him face-to-face; he had looked into those eyes. The man may have hankered after women but not to destroy them. Far from it, he adored them, albeit in a rather self-congratulating way.

The problem with the case was that the murders had happened quickly, and Macleod believed there was no single participant between them. He swore there was a different killer to each one. Almost like a blueprint, like people were told how to do it and then they just didn't quite do it precisely. Similar to a cookery show on TV; they all started with the same ingredients but none of those soufflés matched.

Jane liked the cooking on TV. She'd watch those shows endlessly. The good part was she'd come up with a recipe idea and he'd get to sample her efforts, and often they were very good. He was missing that currently, for after discussion, she had left to go abroad for a short while after Clarissa had come to him, urged him to get back on the case, albeit in an unofficial way. Jane had offered to help.

She could drive, she could take notes. 'And she could get in the way and end up getting herself hurt or worse,' Macleod had said. He didn't often come down hard against her, but he was not budging from this. Nobody really knew what you faced in this job unless you did it. A lot of people thought they were ready for it until it happened to them. If Jane got attacked, she couldn't defend herself. Macleod and Clarissa were awkward enough given their age but at least they'd had training and often they could see circumstances happening, take evasive action, control the situation. Yes, Jane was better, even if she fretted, she was better away.

The bizarre thing was that Clarissa and Macleod were now staying in many hotels but often operating out of the same room. It would be a bit obvious if two old people kept pitching up in a green car and taking separate rooms. You'd have to explain why; the cover would be more awkward. The idea they were an old couple on a tour of the countryside made a lot more sense. It also cut against what people would think Macleod would do. Clarissa had said to him, 'You've got to be different. If you go undercover, you've got to not be Macleod.' The easiest thing to do was to change your standards.

His thoughts were snapped back to the present as the door opposite him opened and a blast of chilly air came through. Clarissa plonked herself in the driver's seat, handing him a coffee, and placed her own in front of her on the dash.

'I had to walk for that,' she said. 'I had to walk down the street. They had that machine in the supermarket place but no, I went down, and I got this coffee from a proper barista, just before they closed. I hope you're appreciative of that.'

Macleod could feel her nagging at him. 'Of course, I'm appreciative of it,' he said. 'I'm appreciative of everything. All I said was the car was a little small.'

'You'll not get a better car than this,' said Clarissa. 'Als loves this car. Ross has a large smile on his face when he gets in this car with me.'

'Ross looks terrified when he gets in this car with you,' said Macleod, 'and I understand why. 'Some of the . . .'

'Shut it, Seoras. Just shut it. I'm out on a limb here. You're looking at an end of career—I'm not. And I could just go and put my feet up somewhere because this leg is killing me. Do you know something? I just walked down the street to pick up your coffee with a sore leg, so a little bit less attitude.'

Macleod laughed because he knew she wasn't really having a go. She was just laying into him like she always did.

'I'm appreciative of you, and of the other two, you know that, but I hate to say it, I think we're out of luck at the moment. I don't think Winston Arnold is coming back.'

A phone rang and Clarissa dove between her legs to search in her handbag and pull out her mobile.

'Yeah,' said Clarissa. 'Yeah, he still is. No, still looking. Well, we're not surprised about that, are we?'

Macleod looked over at her, urging her to put on the speaker, but Clarissa shook her head. 'We'll see. Get you some idea. Yes. Looking as if we might have to do something different. The leg, grumbling, but holding up.'

Macleod scowled; that was never about her leg; that was her talking about him to Hope. Clarissa soon closed down the call, but Macleod sat in anticipation of what had been said.

'Well, you're all ears,' said Clarissa.

'What's happening? What's happening? We've been sat here most of the day. We've got a guy who doesn't turn up, and now you get a phone call from the only other two people we know who could actually get this job done. What's happening?'

'Well, Hope says not much at their end. They're still talking about Ian Lamb as being the killer. There's an investigation going on into how he managed to commit suicide, but Ross is coming up with nothing else either. He's tried looking into Winston Arnold, into the bookshop. There's nothing online that's pulling him down or indicating where he's gone if he's not here. I think it's coming to that point, Seoras.'

4

'Did you try the butcher again?'

'I tried the butcher. I went in. The guy tried to sell me a couple of steaks, which I was very, very tempted to take on your money.'

'My money's paying for the hotel.'

'And the last one wasn't great, was it? And you snore.'

Macleod almost looked incredulous, but he shook his head. 'So, what are they doing?'

'Just getting on with it. The body beneath the bridge gave us nothing, apparently. Jona says it's the same as before—no DNA, nothing. The method of dispatch looks similar. Still got all the symbols on the child. Doesn't appear to be a connection or an obvious tie at least, other than the symbols themselves. None of the children killed knew each other. They're far apart. They're not of a particular colour, a particular hair type, eyes, anything like that; they're just all single mums with young kids. It's tragic, Seoras; it's tragic.'

'It's more than tragic. There's something else going on,' said Macleod. 'That's the thing. Something is pulling these people together.'

'Well, we're not going to find it sitting here,' said Clarissa. 'Drink your coffee up. I think we'll head back to the hotel. We're going to have to break into there tonight.'

Macleod looked over at her.

'What?' she said.

'You know I'm not keen on this. It's not how I operate.'

'No, you get a warrant. Something akin to that. You get into the place through legal means; we don't have legal means. We're working on the edge here.'

'I've never worked outside the law,' said Macleod. 'I've always followed it. I've always toed the line.'

'Well, the line isn't there anymore and some of these kids are going to die. You said yourself it's not going to stop. You'd said yourself that they've gone quiet because the wrong person's been strung up, giving them time to regroup. You said it's in your blood, it's not going away, so unless you can somehow miraculously get your job back, or somehow offer some reasonable evidence that allows Hope to come in here and kick that door down, you and I are going to break in there and find out what Winston Arnold's got in his place.'

Macleod sat back in the chair. He put the coffee to his lips, drank it, and listened to the rain tapping down on top.

'Do you want to look around the place in daylight?'

'What do you mean look around the place?' asked Macleod. 'What good's that going to do?'

'You can see a lot from places in the daylight even if you can't get in; it makes it easier for you when you try to get in.'

'You talk like you did this for a living, like you broke into places.'

'Well, in the art world, sometimes you have to find out about stuff.'

'Yes, and last time you tried to find out about stuff, you jumped on the roof and fell down and you've now got that leg busted up which is not going to be helpful if we have to clear out of here in a hurry tonight.'

'We're not going to be clearing out in a hurry,' said Clarissa, 'because nobody's going to know we're in. I'm going to take a look around the building, see if I can see any alarms and that.'

'And what are you going to do if there's an alarm?'

'Disable it. You just cut the red wire, don't you?' He took the bait before he realised what she was doing and watched as her face burst into laughter. 'Lighten up, Seoras, lighten up. We'll

6

just pop in into somebody's shop to have a look around.'

'I'm not happy about it though.'

'I didn't ask you to be happy,' said Clarissa, 'but if we don't find out where this is going, if we don't pull something out of the hat, it's going to start again, and in your current capacity, you're not going to be able to do it by wholly legal means.'

Macleod sighed and watched as she drained the last of her cup of coffee, putting it back on the dash before stepping outside. As he watched her in the wing mirror of the car, she passed by the shop, peering in as if interested in one of the books in the front window. She then went to walk off but stopped again as if she had a second thought about an object. After that, she walked down the street out of sight, and Macleod reckoned she was at the rear looking for a way in.

They'd agreed that he shouldn't be out of the car more than necessary, especially around places such as this. In the daylight, and with his reputation, he was likely to get spotted. He was no movie star, but he had appeared on the television several times, so he did need to be careful.

Macleod saw a police car at the far end of the village and as it came past, he pulled down a cap he was wearing. It was an old duncher type, one that his father may have worn, or his father, but it did the job of covering up the top half of his face. He only lifted his head again when the police car had driven past. He wondered if this was how it felt for the criminals when he was after them and they didn't want him interfering. Is this how they hid, in plain sight in front of you?

It took Clarissa another twenty minutes before she arrived back at the car. Stepping inside out of the rain, Macleod could see that her shawl was wet, and he turned away as she shook it.

'You're worse than a dog,' he said, and then suddenly stopped himself.

'Is that what you tell Jane as well, refer to her as a dog? Just shut it and let's get on. We need to get you some black clothing. How much have you got?' Macleod glared at her. 'You need to give me sizes. You're not going into the store. That would be the worst decision, going in somewhere looking for a breaking-and-entry outfit.'

He simply nodded this time and drained the rest of his coffee as Clarissa started up the small, green sports car. They'd go find him some clothing, head back to the little guest house they were staying at, have some dinner, and then return to enter Winston Arnold's shop, the first break-in of Macleod's career.

Something about it just didn't feel right but as he watched the woman beside him drive along, he was glad it was her. Clarissa was an old hand; she wasn't dodgy, but she could fight dirty, and he was going to have to fight dirty here. They'd taken away his right to investigate, replaced him with someone who clearly was not understanding the case. If he didn't step up, more bodies would be found. As much as he thought the woman beside him was certifiably mad, he was darn glad to have her.

Chapter 2

Macleod pulled on the hoodie top, struggling to get his arms through, and then pulled his head through the gap at the top. He was a man of shirts and although when he wore the occasional cardigan, everything was buttoned up the front. Nothing was pulled over the top like this.

'It's clearly not you, is it? There's no way anyone's going to think that's you.'

'I don't think it's me,' said Macleod. He pulled a balaclava over the top of his head. It was of a light material, and it only showed his eyes when he allowed the front section to be pulled up towards his nose.

'Now pull the hoodie up with it,' said Clarissa.

He did so and looked in the mirror. Something about it reviled him. He felt a tap on his shoulder and his hoodie was pulled back down and the balaclava pulled down to around his neck. She handed him the long black raincoat that would go around and over the top, and he agreed that he simply looked like an old man out for a walk when it was done up over the top of the hoodie. The hood part had disappeared down inside the top of the coat, and he felt more like himself.

'You ready for this?' she said, with a sudden serious look on her face.

'We're getting past the alarms how?' asked Macleod. 'You never said that.'

'That's because he doesn't have any alarms. The back door is locked pathetically. It won't take me long to open it at all. It's just a standard key.'

'Since when did you become such an expert in opening doors?'

'You have to be. Well, you need to know the basics. I couldn't do it if it's a decent door, but I could certainly do this one.'

'And if you couldn't, what was the plan?'

'Smash a window, get in that way.'

'With your foot?'

'Well, you'd be going first', said Clarissa. 'You can't expect a woman in my condition to be climbing around.'

Macleod had seen the condition of her foot. It was heavily bruised and every time she stood on it, he could see her fighting not to swear, but Clarissa was nothing, if not determined. She wasn't called his Rottweiler for no reason.

The pair made their way out, arm in arm, past the owner of the guest house and into Clarissa's little green car before driving it to just off the main street of the village where Winston Arnold's bookshop stood. There was a light rain as they got out and together they strolled arm in arm down the pavement until they cut up through an alleyway towards the back of the shop.

As they got closer, Clarissa reached down inside Macleod's coat, pulled the hood out, and told him to slip the balaclava on. He did so, grabbed the hood and took it over the top of his head and turned to see her similarly dressed in black. She wore a black scarf around her face rather than a balaclava for there was no containing her hair. She did, however, have another hood going over the top, and like him, you could just about see her eyes.

The back gate to the shop and flat combination owned by Winston Arnold was a latch affair and opened easily. Once they'd snuck inside, Macleod stood at the gate listening while Clarissa went over to the door ready to break in. She opened it gently, pushed the door, and then turned around and through whispered teeth told him to follow her. Once inside, they took a moment to allow their eyes to adjust to the darkness.

'You'll need to search the store,' she said to Macleod. 'I'll go upstairs, check out the living quarters, see what else I can find there. Remember to keep your gloves on.'

Macleod nodded, snapped on the evidence gloves that would be used to stop any contamination of the scene. They quickly walked along, looking through racks of books. He was taken aback by a sudden large sign that said Satanism. He almost swayed from the large letters in front of his face, especially when he saw the number of books, but there were other books on other cultures, other faiths and religions. Many of the books seemed to indicate a dark side. He flipped through them quickly, taking each book, seeing if anything was loose inside, but when nothing showed, he started looking through the cupboards of the shop.

The very front of the shop was difficult to get to because streetlights lit up the interior to some degree, and anyone walking past would not be visible until they got to the shop front. Macleod could easily have been seen, so he remained rooted in the rear of the shop, scrambling around, lifting this and that.

Towards the rear of the shop there seemed to be a more private collection of books. There was no label and each one seemed different. Maybe it was the second-hand tomes to get rid of, maybe he just didn't recognise any of these books. Macleod started pulling them out until he found one with a number of Post-it Notes sticking out of it. The yellow markers were twisted and frayed as if they'd been used for quite a while.

When Macleod put the book in front of him, peering as best he could at the text, he realised it was all about symbology. As he flipped through the book he saw Mayan, Aztec, and Egyptian symbols. There was no symbol identification for anything satanic which Macleod thought was interesting. As he flicked through the pages, a loose page slipped out, wafting towards the floor. He closed the symbology book, put it back on the shelf, and picked up the paper.

There were a number of symbols on it. It certainly was no alphabet he was used to. Quickly, he took out his notebook and started writing down what was on the page. He'd have to be quick, get the page back in, because they couldn't hang around long, could they?

Or could they? After all, if there was no alarm and it was only eleven o'clock at night, so maybe they could. They could have all night in here. Who was likely to come? Unless Winston Arnold managed to make it back, there wouldn't be a problem.

He replaced the sheet back inside the symbology book, returned it to the shelf, and continued his search. There were plenty more books, many of them showing sacrifices and rituals of different religions, but he didn't have the time to scan through them all. He certainly didn't come across one that said, 'We take a small child and carve symbols into him.' There was no mention of single mothers.

Macleod nearly jumped when a hiss came from behind him, 'Seoras, up here, come on.'

He followed Clarissa up small wooden steps to an apartment above. He could see though the light was dim, that there was a small kitchenette unit and living room. Another room was located to one side, and it was to here that Clarissa walked, opening the door, and telling Macleod to crouch down. Once inside, he realised why. The streetlights lit up the room and she'd dare not move in front of the window at full height. Macleod stared around though. There were a number of pictures and posters on the wall. Clarissa looked over at one, pointed to a painting.

'That's impressive, it's probably worth about four hundred quid.'

'What?' queried Macleod and he looked at it. 'Someone's being decapitated in that picture.'

'Yeah. Even the art world's got its weird side. Well, actually it's got a lot of weird sides, but that particular picture, Portuguese, and in certain art circles that would go down a treat. I think it's part of an entire set, but they've never been all pulled together. Yeah, I would say about four hundred quid. The painter was a nut job.'

Macleod couldn't believe his ears, and he looked round at other symbols within the room. He noted that below the window line, a lot of the symbols and pictures were grosser. There were no upside-down crosses above the window line. Pictures of visceral cuttings, stomachs being opened, made him feel like he was in a dungeon museum. Part of his stomach began to churn.

'Definitely crackpot, eh? I bet you he kept this place locked up. I mean, downstairs, I guess is what, just mainly books and that?'

'Books and rites and rituals and all that stuff,' said Macleod, 'but I mean, it's just books, it's not like this.' He saw a computer on the far side. 'Don't suppose we can get into that,' he said.

'No way,' said Clarissa. 'We're getting in, we're getting out, we are not going hunting for files. That's beyond my remit here. We do that, we're liable to get caught having gone in or alert him that we've gone online. We don't want to do that either.'

'Of course not,' said Macleod. 'Of course not.'

Clarissa walked forward on her knees and saw a picture that was below waist height. It was on the wall and Macleod saw it as several people being crucified in a rather bizarre fashion.

'He is a collector,' she said, 'but that's a dark collection. You don't see these things going into auction houses. More like the black, weird market, so to speak. I mean, there's nothing illegal in it, and it's fairly disgusting, but as a picture, it's not something you really want to be known for having. You're collecting it for different reasons, shall we say.'

'What about the rest of the place? Have you tried that living room?'

'It's not easy, you're going to have to do it on the belly,' she said. 'In case you didn't realise, I'm not built to be crawling around on my belly.'

'We'd best have a look in there though.'

Together, they crawled out on their knees into the short landing corridor and Macleod stepped into the kitchenette at the back, staying low. 'I'll search here. You take the front.'

'You take the front,' said Clarissa. 'You have to get down lower in the front, it's easier to see in. There's nothing round the back to look in from.'

Macleod nodded reluctantly and went to the front of the house. On his belly, he crawled in and saw a TV at the front of the small lounge. There was a rather attractive sofa, and as he crawled across the carpet on his knees and elbows, he saw a collection of horror DVDs in the wall. He opened several cupboards, but there wasn't much there. Macleod got the feeling that Winston Arnold's true delight was in the study room and in his shop below.

He stopped, wondering about this man. *Did he kill? Was he the one that botched it up? Where was he now? Had they come for him because he'd screwed things up, or was he off after someone else?* Macleod had the coded note and he'd need to sit down and work on it, although in reality, he wasn't banking on getting an answer.

'Seoras, bugger, Seoras.'

'What?' he said and turned around on his hands and knees to see Clarissa peering in from the door.

'There's a bloody alarm in here. The bloody alarm's gone off.'

'I can't hear an alarm.'

'It's bloody silent. Come on, get your arse out of here.'

Macleod crawled as quickly as his knees and arms would allow him back out into the corridor and then followed Clarissa down the steps. From the back of the shop, they could see blue lights at the front on the road.

'Bollocks,' said Clarissa, and she made for the back door peering out quickly. 'They're not here yet, come on.'

She opened the door, Macleod stepped out, and she closed it behind her. Macleod could hear her locking it as he stepped towards the small gate at the back. He was about to open it when he could hear footsteps outside on the path. Looking around, he wondered what to do but Clarissa was already over, looking at some bins.

She opened them up, looked inside and then pointed at him, telling him to get in. There was a handy stump, an old relic of a tree that had been cut away back down to as small as possible. He helped her up onto it and then into the furthest bin. He then stepped up, put his foot in as he heard the gate beginning to open. His hand remained up high, catching the lid as it came down, allowing it to close softly.

Macleod's heart was thumping. He couldn't get caught doing this. He'd be out of a job. He remembered, he was out of a job already anyway, but they could get a criminal record. How do you explain being in a bin at the back of somebody's house with an alarm going off? He sat tight in the bin wondering what Clarissa was thinking. She was making no sound and he thought he'd best do the same.

Macleod could hear someone at the back door of the shop. They were turning it this way and that way, and then speaking into a radio saying that it seemed like a false alarm because everything was secure. Ideas were thrown up of mice setting off the alarm, other animals getting in; birds, possibly down a chimney, though Macleod couldn't remember a chimney being on the building. Either way, the police officer seemed extremely relaxed and when his partner came round, she agreed with him, and they reported there have been no signs of disturbance.

Macleod sat tight as he heard them disappear out through the gate at the rear. He wondered when Clarissa would deem it safe to move. It was over an hour before Clarissa did anything, and when she did, he heard the thump of a bin falling forward and then heard her muted cries of pain. The lid of his bin was

16

opened up about ten seconds later.

'Come on, got to get out of here. Bloody ankle.' She wasn't waiting for him or helping him out of the bin. Instead, she was at the gate turning the latch and telling him to come. He managed to scrabble out of his bin, half toppling at the same time, and he pulled it back upright closing from the lid down, helping hers back to its original position as well.

'Seoras, get the hell out,' she said through clenched teeth.

That was nice, he thought, *she just said my name.* He raced over to the gate, closing it behind him, and then pulled down his hoodie and his balaclava, putting his arm around her, underneath her shoulder as she limped along. He removed her scarf and hood, and together the two of them tried to look like an elderly couple who, for some reason, were out walking in the late hours of night. When they reached the green sports car, she hobbled round to the passenger side.

'Don't you bloody well scratch it, let's get back. Remember to act as if you're half pissed when we get in.'

'What? Why are we acting like we're drunk?' asked Macleod.

'Because that guy in the guest house will be up. I want him to think we've just been out for a few bevs. You do know how to act drunk, don't you?'

Macleod had never been drunk in his life. Alcohol was the demon's drink. He had no idea, though he had seen many a criminal give a good impersonation. He'd do his best. As he drove off, he thought to himself, *But I'm driving. I'd have to be half sober*.

Chapter 3

'Did he say much more?'

Hope looked up from her coffee at the concerned face of her colleague DC Ross. Usually, Ross was an amiable sort of fellow but due to recent events, there was starting to become a darker side to him. Hope was well capable of tossing out the sarky comment to the DCI in light of his actions, but she also knew how to pitch it best. It wasn't in Ross's nature to have a go at people and yet clearly the frustration of having had his boss taken away from him, unfairly as Ross saw it, was making him rather grumpy.

'I think they're going to have to break into that building. Winston Arnold hasn't turned up and I get the feeling that Clarissa's going to have to pull the boss into a side of life he doesn't particularly enjoy. In fact, I'm not even sure he's even done anything like that before.'

Ross's face showed no sign of improvement. 'It's not right. It's not right, and he wasn't wrong either. Ian Lamb, with what's happened to him, some of that's got to go on the DCI.'

'Don't fret about the DCI,' said Hope. 'You keep your head down. That's how you best help Macleod. Not having a go at anyone. Leave the sarky quips to me, I'm good at that. I'm good at handling people in that way. You be yourself, Alan. The guy building a team up, the guy that holds it together, the guy that's always got a smile. Don't let the anger take you down.'

'Well, it's not damn well right, is it? If they can do that to him, they could do that to any of us. What's the past count for? He's solved how many cases? Got on top of how many things? Even the ones he couldn't prosecute, he's always got them. He's always been able to see what's going on, and worse than that, we're sitting waiting for the next victim, totally unawares.'

'Just be thankful we're still getting to investigate even though they're calling it a wrap-up. Even if we're just saying we want to understand Ian Lamb better, as long as there's some sort of an open file at the moment, that keeps us right where we want to be. We don't want to lose that.'

'Of course not, it just stinks.'

Hope almost laughed. Ross couldn't do the angry person very well. He should have sworn, tipped up the table, thrown the chair across the room, but instead, he just looked like a mildly annoyed Sunday school teacher when the naughty children had pulled a prank on him.

He was also still worried about the application to adopt a child. Hope knew it hadn't gone smoothly so far and it clearly was bothering the man, for he rarely spoke of it. Something as joyous as that, Ross would have shared it, would have talked about it. She also felt he was missing Clarissa. Hope was Ross's direct boss. Clarissa, while being a grade above, was more of an equal to Ross. The bottom end of the office.

It happened wherever you were. As soon as you got any sort of rank, as soon as you moved up a bit, the people down below didn't associate with you the same way. They might still like you; they might even think you're a good boss, but it was never the same. In Clarissa, Alan Ross had a foot soldier to stand by and a quirkier character he was unlikely to meet. But Clarissa was where she needed to be, assisting the boss, showing him how to get things done when you didn't have the full authority of the law behind you, when you had to go into the wild side.

Seoras had once told her that Clarissa could fight dirty, that Clarissa was an old hand and understood a lot about the things that they never wrote in the textbooks. He said Hope should keep an eye on her, watch how she operates at times but never pick up that cursed attitude. Hope had laughed at that one.

What she was finding hard was not speaking to Macleod, everything rooting through Clarissa, so it would never be picked up that they were talking to Macleod. He was away, away off out of the country avoiding all the press. At least that's what they told everyone. They got Jane out and now Macleod and Clarissa were touring, chasing down the leads that Hope wasn't allowed to go on.

'Sombre today?' Hope looked up. Jona Nakamura was standing at the table.

'I can't usually sneak up on you two, can I?'

'I hope you've got something good,' said Hope, 'because we could do with a shot in the arm. Everything just seems to be so down and we're going nowhere. Struggling to even go and work on the case.'

'I take it he's not out of the country then.'

'What do you mean?' asked Hope. Her face impassive.

Jona sat down, pulled a chair up close to Hope, and said quietly, 'The boss, Macleod; he's not out of the country, is he? You forget I used to do meditation sessions with him. I understand the man. They've gone beyond the pale this

20

time with him. They've pushed him beyond the limit. All he needed was a trigger, a trigger to buck up. He looked down and defeated, but there's a killer on the loose and that's him. That's his core, saving the innocent. He wouldn't have sat away from it. It would have ripped him apart.'

'I have no idea what you mean,' said Hope, sarcastically.

'Off with the Rottweiler, is he?' said Jona smiling. 'But hey, I've been thinking, we looked at the DNA that was associated with Sandra Mackie. I know the killer slept with her, but he also didn't leave a trace. I'm a bit astounded by that but, of course, the family DNA, that's what we should be looking at if we believe that somebody slept with her.'

'What do you mean?' said Hope.

'Of course,' said Ross. 'If it was a sibling. If it was someone close in the family. If we didn't get a great match.'

'Ross is right,' said Jona. 'DNA sampling and that, it's not always easy to get a match, but it would be much more difficult if the DNA was so close to begin with.'

'You think one of her family slept with her? Yuck,' said Hope. 'That's sick.'

'We're talking about people that carve symbols on to dead children,' said Jona. 'I don't think we should rule out any level of sickness.'

Ross stood up. 'And where are you going?' asked Hope.

'I'll find them, find the members of the family. I'll go check them out.'

'Under what basis?' said Hope.

'Just dotting the i's and crossing the t's, trying to understand Sandra Mackie's lifestyle, why the women were all chosen. Something like that. Anyway, if somebody comes asking, you're the one who can do the sarky. You're the one who can handle that.'

Hope raised the finger. 'Don't! Don't throw my words back at me. That was the pep talk from heaven.' Ross smiled, gave a little laugh, and turned, leaving the canteen.

'How are you guys holding up?' asked Jona.

'Well, it's different; he's not the greatest to work for—the DCI.'

'He certainly isn't. I feel like I'm explaining everything three times over to him. Seoras was never like that. Seoras just took what I said.'

'If he didn't, you told him off for it. It's not easy,' said Hope. 'The boss wasn't just the boss; he was a friend. We got used to each other. Lawson is something else; he still can't see that Ian Lamb was innocent.'

'Well, we can't prove it, can we? Too many things line up with him.'

'All coincidental. You can't take the suicide as an idea that he's guilty; could have just been the whole pressure he was under. Seoras was trying to prevent that. That's why he wanted him out and released early. To give the impression that we didn't think anything of him.'

'But he did, didn't he?'

'Seoras didn't believe he did it, but he always kept it on the back burner that he could be wrong. I mean you have to, but he's soon going to find out.'

'Wish him all the best then. Anything I can do?' asked Jona.

'I don't speak to him, talking only to Clarissa. We have to . . . we need to be careful. He can't be seen doing anything. Can't be seen running around doing an investigation when he's been taken off the case.'

'I guess she can't either. Why's she not here?'

22

'Oh, the foot's played up; it's really bad. She got signed off for several weeks.'

'She's some operator,' said Jona, 'but I'm going back to where I hide out. If Lawson wants me, I'll send one of my deputies.'

Hope laughed, but the situation wasn't good. She went to finish off her coffee, but as she put the cup down on the table, she suddenly saw her new boss coming through the doors of the canteen.

'Hope,' he said, 'I need you up in the office now.'

'I'm just finishing the coffee.'

'I need you now; I really need you.'

Hope could hear the sniggers across the canteen. What way was that to phrase it? She lifted her cup, putting it on the rack at the side before following Lawson out of the door and making her way up the stairs to his office. Once inside, he showed her to her seat and then took up a position behind his own desk.

Has his seat been raised? she thought. Two days ago, when she'd been in here, even though she was sitting, she was able to look down at him when he was behind his desk, but the seat had been raised so they were now on a level. Hope understood that her height, and given the fact she was a woman, sometimes intimidated smaller men, but she was struggling not to laugh at this attempt to equalise their height.

'How are things going, Sergeant? Oh sorry. I should say Hope, shouldn't I? I sometimes think I should give you the term, sergeant. It's great to see a woman of your age up at that rank.'

Hope wondered if this was the greatest backhand compliment ever. *A woman at that rank; there are plenty of female sergeants. What was he seeking?*

'I'm still working on tying up some loops. It'll be a wee while longer. Ross is doing a little bit of work on Sandra Mackie's family. We're just trying to see if there was a real connection between the women. With Ian Lamb dead, obviously it's hard to know.'

'Yes, well, not that it matters. He'll not be killing any more people. Kids will be safe.'

'If it was him,' said Hope.

'Oh, it's not him? There's been no more killings. Clearly, it was him. You're going to have to accept that Macleod got it wrong; the man's old. We all lose it at some point. You maybe don't get that, being young and dynamic. You really do cut a great image.'

Hope sat back in her seat. She was never bothered that men would look at her. As long as they didn't stare for too long, she simply took it as a compliment. She was an imposing figure; she was tall, but she was also a good detective, something that Macleod reminded her constantly. He had owned up to the way he'd seen her at first. The fact that he was quite taken with her, but he always gave her credit for what she did, credit for the detective she was, and pushed her for the one she could become.

'Macleod's not coming back. Or at least, it's extremely doubtful,' said Lawson, 'and I think this force could do with a new female DI. You've been the face behind Macleod for so long. I can see you out there handling the press; you've done that before. In fact, I'm told by some of the press people that they'd rather deal with you than Macleod. Much more pleasant to talk to.'

'And much more pleasant to look at,' said Hope.

'Yes, much more pleasant to look at.'

Hope stared, her eyes penetrating into the man's mind until it dawned on him what he'd just said.

'Not that that is a reason for you to be there. It's your detective work that does it.'

'Of course,' said Hope. 'I never thought anything different.'

'Well,' the man coughed slightly, 'I think what I'm trying to say is, have you thought about going for detective inspector? You'd be good at it. You could run this team, and if you didn't want Clarissa, we can move her on; she's not far from retirement. Ross is good, dynamic. Also good for the figures.'

Hope went to shake her head. Ross was just good. Who cared what orientation he was. The figures never came into it. Who was she kidding? Figures always came into it. Always things had to be seen to be this or to be that. Macleod was old school. You just solved the darn case.

'Thinking that I should come in and take over. I'm not the only DS here.'

'Clarissa Urquhart?' said the man, almost joking. 'You've got to be kidding. At least Macleod kept some sort of a rein on her. Have you spoken to any of the art people about what she's like?'

'I don't have to,' said Hope. 'I work with her.'

'Yes, well, she's not DI material. She never has been, and besides, I think you'd look better up in that position than her. Have a think about it,' said the man. He stood up from behind his desk, walked round to the front of it, and then tried to manoeuvre his bottom as he sat on it. 'The thing is, Hope . . .'

Lawson fell off the desk. Hope smiled, tried not to laugh, and then stood up and reached down for the man, her height emphasised as he was lying on the floor.

'I'll take it under advisement,' said Hope. 'We'll try and see

25

if we can come up with something in the case, some sort of explanation of what was going on.'

'Good. Good,' said Lawson, brushing himself down, 'and not a word to anyone about this. I'll see if I can fast-track you.'

'I haven't said I'm doing it yet,' said Hope, striding over to the office door.

'You should wear your hair down, especially around the office,' said Lawson; 'good image to have.'

Hope reached up to the side of her neck and her fingers traced up to where the ponytail came at the back of her hand. 'I'm a practical person,' said Hope; 'this is the most practical way to wear my hair. Doesn't really work to have it flying around my face if I'm chasing someone down.'

'Of course not. Of course not. Anyway, think on it.'

'Of course, Alan,' said Hope, and she closed the door behind her. If he knew anything about her, the one thing she wouldn't be was someone's puppet. She'd be an inspector one day but on her terms and in her time.

Chapter 4

Clarissa's head was swimming as she tried to process the tips she'd been given along with where she was to meet someone. Talking to her colleagues in the art world, one had arranged for her to meet up with a rather dubious collector, but he in turn sent her elsewhere. No, she was to meet a man—a Greek man—who may have known something about the transport of the ornamental knives to the UK. Hopefully, the same knives that were used to cut into the children.

It was a bit of a long shot on an overheard rumour. She wasn't quite sure who the Greek man was. She'd heard his name before, but she wasn't even sure that was his name. Was it his? Was it somebody he worked with? You could never tell with these things. It had meant an early start and her foot was currently killing her. The idea of letting Macleod drive was not one she found palatable and so she'd strapped her leg up, put the boot on, and driven up with Seoras in the passenger seat, constantly reminding her that he could drive if she wanted.

They'd headed from the borders up to Gourock, just to the west of Glasgow, and in particular, to Battery Park. It was a wide open space looking out onto the Clyde, and today it was chilly. That was nothing unusual. Glasgow could be quite windy and out here by the open water when a fresh breeze was blowing, it sent the cold through to your bones. As she parked the car, she wasn't sure just how she would take to the weather outside, but she reached into the rear of her car and pulled out her shawl. Stepping outside, she wrapped herself up in it. Then it came close to her, and she could feel the heaviness of it, but also the warmth.

Walking around to the passenger side, she tapped the window so Macleod rolled it down, and she crouched slightly so she could look at him face to face.

'I think it's best if I go alone. These types, they won't like it if you pitch up with too many people. Even worse if you get some sort of amateur like yourself.' Macleod raised an eyebrow. 'Amateur in terms of the art world, I mean. That's why I'm here. It's what I'm meant to be doing. To turn up with another copper, who doesn't understand the business. Well, I'm not even meant to be a copper at the moment; I'm meant to be meeting this man on the off chance of looking out for these knives.'

'That's fine. I've got the code on the bit of paper I found. I'll sit and do it. I'll keep an eye on you though.'

'What's going to happen here, Seoras? Look around us, Battery Park. There are mums with pushchairs, kids. Safest place you could be.'

'Nowhere is ever safe. Not when you're chasing down information like this,' said Macleod. 'It's not like we just call back up. Just be careful.'

Clarissa nodded and turned around, her shawl sweeping against the window and possibly even touching his face through it. *Macleod's worrying too much*, she thought and began to hobble forward. She needed to work on that. Biting her tongue, she tried to walk smoothly and hoped she gave a good impression because her ankle was killing her.

It wasn't difficult to spot the man she was going to talk to in Battery Park. One of the key things of turning up in a large location like this was to make sure you looked like you had a purpose. He didn't. He looked like someone looking for someone. He was old, older than she, and she could see his feet tapping and the hands shaking.

'Are you a man who can do a deal?' asked Clarissa.

The man looked at her. 'Depends what you're looking for.'

'I'm looking for knives. Ornate ones, but knives?' The man looked here and there. 'Easy,' said Clarissa. 'What's the problem? Maybe we should sit down on that bench.'

'Why do you want to sit on the bench?' asked the man.

'So we actually look like two people who've met and are sitting for a chat as opposed to two people randomly standing in the middle of a kid's play park and looking all around them as if they're about to be attacked.'

The man nodded, sat down quickly, and Clarissa plonked herself on the bench beside him. It was cold. The wind was biting, and she watched the kids with envy as they ran around. If she could run around at that speed, she might be vaguely warm. No, she'd be vaguely warmer but still cold.

'What happened to the knives?' asked Clarissa. 'My contact said that you might be able to lead me to them.'

'The knives, yes,' said the man, his eyes again scanning all around. 'The thing is, it's my nephew. He was looking into the knives, the transportation of them. There were twelve. Pretty nice set, strange set, strange markings.'

'When are they from?' asked Clarissa.

'Possibly fifteenth century. They have some significance in certain religions, I think.'

'What sort of religions?'

'Well, I said religion, anti-religion. Possibly Satanism.'

'Oh,' said Clarissa trying to look surprised but instead, the hairs on her neck jumped up. She might be onto something.

'There were twelve of them.'

'Yes. Some sort of connection between them. They came as a set. Anyway, my nephew was doing the transportation. They were in a private collection in West Wales before my nephew got them, but there was so much heat attached to them, especially now.'

'Why so much heat?'

'You've seen the killings. These were torture knives or carving knives. Knives that could inflict pain or mark the skin.'

'Right,' said Clarissa, 'and rare, I take it. But why would you think they're attached to these killings? It's an art piece, isn't it?'

'I owed him a favour. Okay, I have done my favour.' The man was referring to Clarissa's contact. 'I came here,' he said, 'because if I didn't, you would come to me. Everyone knows you, your collections, what you do.'

Clarissa hoped that he was referring to her cover name in the art world and not the fact she was a detective solving a murder. 'You would come to my house, you would hunt me down. When you want something, you'd get it so I'm here to tell you, okay? I don't want my family and my home exposed, neither my nephew. You asked; I have told. Now I go.'

'You haven't told me that much,' said Clarissa. 'You haven't told me how I'd get hold of them. You haven't told me who they've gone to.'

'My nephew won't tell who they've gone to either. Best forget about them. Best not look too closely, especially if they're being . . .'

'Being what?' asked Clarissa.

'If they have anything to do with those children, you don't want to be involved.'

Oh yes, I do, thought Clarissa. *I want to be deeply involved and I want to find out where they are*. Instead, she held her peace and stood up with the man shaking his hand. She watched him disappear, his grey overcoat pulled up tight, but his bald head severely exposed to the wind. *He must be freezing*, she thought. Clarissa looked around, but she couldn't see anyone watching the man, no one watching her. If anybody had stumbled across their meeting, they were doing a good job of not showing it.

She went back towards the car, rapped the window when she saw that Macleod was deeply engaged in his paper, or rather the sheet of paper that had the codes on that was being held up inside his newspaper. The window rolled down.

'Much use?'

'Not really. I know that the knives came in from his nephew. Originally in West Wales. There's a set of twelve cutting knives. Knives for marking the skin. Possibly satanic.'

'Well, that's a start. Who's his nephew?'

'I'll need to get my contact to run that through. I don't know. I don't know these people but that would make sense. You wouldn't run some of these knives through some of the better collectors. Everyone would know about it soon. You'd be a mug to do that. How's your code going anyway?'

'You said that you had a professor who did symbols, didn't you?'

31

'Yes. Why?'

'I'm wondering if she could help with this, but on the other hand . . .'

'What, Seoras?'

'If it's a coded message, are you going to have people who can read the symbols? How clever are these people? Maybe there's just a code to follow to put it into English.'

Clarissa gave a shiver, walked around the back of the car, and got in beside Macleod. 'Give us a look at them,' she said and snatched the paper causing Macleod to tut.

'It's not that simple,' he said. 'You need to think this one through. You're not just going to look at it.'

Clarissa scanned the first set of symbols. They repeated a few times as did another one. Some were circles and they looked like figures, some had an image of a sun, one of them the image of a hill. *Was that a donkey? No, it couldn't have been a donkey*, she thought. *I don't know what that one is.*

She handed the paper back to Macleod. 'No bloody idea, Seoras. I'll get you the professor's number if you want.'

'You probably best not,' he said. 'The fewer people we involve at the moment directly from ourselves the better. I might send it up to Ross, but he is going to have to work on it on the quiet. Maybe I'll just go at it myself.'

Clarissa watched him write down letters underneath the symbols. Then large pen strokes went through those letters as he changed them into other letters.

'What are you doing?' she asked.

'If you assume that the symbols are certain letters and then you can cross-reference the letter and you can get the rest of the message, but you've got to set the code up so it all makes sense, which is quite hard. Though it is a long message, I think

32

there's detailed instructions here, but I need to break the code to understand what is written.'

'Not with you,' said Clarissa. 'I am not with you.'

'It's all right,' replied Macleod. 'You're not bad as a driver.'

Clarissa gave him a dig with her elbow. 'Over there, Seoras,' she said. 'That's the Greek guy I was talking to. What do you make of him?'

Macleod looked over. 'He seems very nervy. You would just come out and talk about a deal. You think these knives are putting a bit of a strain on people and things are going on with them that we don't know about?'

'Could be. Could be in this world. I think we should follow him, see where he goes and maybe get led back to his nephew.'

'That's an idea,' said Macleod. 'That's a good idea. Tell you what? Let's get out on foot for a minute to see where he goes locally, see if he jumps on the bus.'

'All right,' said Clarissa, 'but it's blooming cold out there.'

She stepped out again into the chill air and watched as Macleod stepped out, showing no signs at all of being bothered by it. He had a large raincoat on and had brought a hat with a rather broad brim, and she thought he looked like a disappointing cowboy or one of those enforcers in the movies. Somehow the physique just didn't quite match up.

Together they walked along, Clarissa putting her arm in his, completing the picture of an older couple. The Greek man walked along the street looking this way and that. Clarissa and Macleod held their ground, remaining well back, cutting up onto the path that ran alongside the Clyde on occasion and watching him from across. The Greek man stopped close to a set of traffic lights and the trailing pair came closer to him, but from behind so he couldn't see them.

'That's enough here,' said Macleod. 'We'll just keep it nice and easy.'

Suddenly the Greek man looked around as if he'd seen something, then made his way out onto the road.

A car at full pelt struck him, lifting the man up into the air and the body crashed down on top of the roof. He fell off the back as the car continued to race on and Clarissa went to race forward towards the now fallen contact. Macleod grabbed her arm and pulled her back.

'No!' he said sharply in her ear. 'We don't. We're undercover. He's just been struck. If that's deliberate, they'll be watching. Somebody will be watching, and we'll be charging into it. We stand at a distance, look horrified, but we don't get involved. We don't get close. We don't rush in.'

'The man could be dead, Seoras.'

'He could be. And there's plenty of people out there that could do a better job with him than we could. Our focus is on stopping this killer, finding these knives, and if we run in now, we'll lose all that. We'll be spotted. Back.'

Clarissa went to push forward and then yelped as that ankle bit into her. 'Away,' said Macleod. 'We step away slowly as if we are in shock.'

'Did you see the . . .'

'. . . speed they hit him at? They spooked him and then somebody took him out,' said Macleod. 'We're on the right trail.'

As the pandemonium continued around the roadside, people rushing in to have a look, some trying to assist, Macleod turned away with Clarissa. 'We need to find his nephew,' said Macleod, 'and fast.'

Chapter 5

Hope walked into the main office and looked across at the side office of Seoras Macleod, which seemed so quiet these last few days. The DCI had told her to take up residence in it as she was basically running the unit. He had decided to remain upstairs, maybe stroking his ego about being on a higher floor, and kept constantly pushing her to take over Seoras's office. She couldn't do that. It was his; that's where his coat hung, the occasional hat he might wear. There was the table where they sat.

That said, they hadn't taken on any new cases, or were wrapping up the old one, and Clarissa was also due to come back. There'd been no rearrangement of the seating. They hadn't even gone in and used the round table that Macleod had used before. Any conversation simply happened by a chair, usually at Ross's desk, because he had his computer there. Even speaking to Jona, they had gone over to her rather than her come in.

Hope didn't have that assurance of just calling Jona up; she didn't feel in charge; she wasn't the boss. That was for the DCI to do. If she wanted Jona, she'd go to her, and besides, it took her out of what was an uncomfortable feeling within the office. Seoras and she had been through so much and she was struggling with a lack of connection. Talking through Clarissa wasn't the same.

John, her partner, had noticed it as well. Hope wasn't herself, like a part of her was missing. She prayed it was a work connection and not something more. Seoras was a friend, a colleague certainly, a mentor, but she had a fondness for him, one that she rarely spoke of to anyone, and she certainly wasn't going to mention it to John.

'Oi, better leave the light on in there.' Hope flicked her head round and saw Ross waving over at her from his computer. 'Come have a look. I've traced the family.'

Hope strode over and stood behind Ross, towering over his seated form.

'It wasn't too difficult to do. I mean they all have birth records and that, but Sandra Mackie had three siblings but I'm not sure how connected she is with any of them. There's a sister, and there's two brothers and I'm not sure if she had any connection with them. I did give her a call, and she said she could not remember where any of them were. I've gone through bills and tracked them. I've got a Kyle Mackie. I called up his workplace, so to speak, sort of a magic shop. Apparently he's a magician. He's at a hall at the moment on the east side of Inverness practising. I've been told he'll be there for a while. We should probably go and try to talk to him first. There's also a Nathan Mackie, but he's a civil servant in the DWP, the Department of Work and Pensions. I haven't done much research on the sister given that it's a man and that.'

'Of course,' said Hope. 'Well, let's go.'

'Are you okay?' asked Ross. 'You're staring over there. You're not the same since you've come back down from seeing his nibs upstairs.'

'He's pushing me to go for DI.'

'Absolutely, I think you'd make a great detective inspector. You should go for it. I mean you've learned so much, you've . . .'

'You don't understand Ross; he wants me to replace Macleod.'

Ross laughed. 'I think the boss wanted you to replace him as well. Just not quite in this fashion.'

There was a slight kerfuffle when Ross went to drive the car, but Hope insisted that she drive. Whenever it was she and Macleod, she always drove, and she found herself rarely in the car with Ross. Clarissa and he would normally arrive at the scene together or come slightly later because they were picking up equipment or they'd race there early. It just seemed to be the way of the team. The two senior officers were much better together as were the two juniors.

Hope was used to driving and the way she was feeling about the conversation with regard to increasing her rank, it gave her an uneasiness that driving seemed to soothe. You didn't have to think when you drove. In fact, sometimes she didn't. Sometimes she just ended up somewhere, but never in an unsafe fashion. The routine things went on around her while the overarching problem floated off.

That was happening with the department at the moment. The overarching problem was floating off. Where was the murderer? It wasn't Ian Lamb. She kept having to remind herself that with every day that went on, that another child wasn't killed. It wasn't Ian Lamb.

Ross pointed her to a hall. The hall was a community project, and parking up in the tarmacked area that had seen better days,

Hope was careful not to leave any of the wheels in the many potholes that plagued it. Stepping out of the car, she led the way over to the main double doors, knocked on them, and then when there was no response, opened the right hand one carefully.

Once inside, she could hear someone talking in the room. He was expounding about magic and the wonder of it, the amazement that he provided for all would-be magic voyeurs. Hope walked to some flimsy doors, pushed them gently, and then saw the back of a man dressed in a large black cloak. He had a top hat on and a wand, black with white ends. Before him was a large box. He clearly was talking to the far wall as if it was some sort of audience. She watched as he took a saw, and then she noticed that there was a head which seemed to move as he began to saw.

'Excuse me. Excuse me.'

'What? What the hell's this? I said I wasn't to be disturbed. Do you realise what you've done? This was a full-time practice. I was timing this, timing this for the act. For God's sake. What is this? Who the hell are you?'

Hope pulled out her warrant card and held it towards the man. 'Detective Sergeant Hope McGrath. This is Detective Constable Alan Ross. We'd like to talk to you. Mr. Mackie.'

'What do you want to talk to me about? That was nothing to do with me. You got it wrong.'

'Who got what wrong?' asked Hope quizzically.

'The revenue. HMRC. It was their fault. They got it wrong. I don't owe them money.'

'Well, I have no idea if you do or don't owe them money, sir. I'm here to talk to you about your sister.'

The man's face went cold. 'Tragedy,' he said. 'Tragic that she lost her little mite, but I don't talk to her. We aren't close. Just saw it in the news; one never likes to lose a child.'

'Have you lost one yourself, sir?' asked Ross.

'No, but I can imagine you wouldn't want to lose one. I think that's very obvious, Constable.'

'Indeed,' said Ross. 'What is it you're doing here?'

'I'm doing magic,' he said. 'It's amazing the power of a conjurer, isn't it? My audience hanging on every last breath.'

'That's a dummy in there, sir, is it?' asked Ross.

'Of course, it's a dummy. I can't get my assistant at this time of the day.'

'Where do you perform?' asked Hope. 'I don't know your name. Maybe I haven't seen you on the circuit.'

'The circuit? I've done cruise ships. I've done everything. I've been around the world.'

'Currently, you're what? Working in Inverness?'

'I am merely taking time out to rehearse and perfect, and then we shall be back at the big stages.'

'Where have you played,' asked Ross, 'If I may ask?'

'Palladium.'

'London?' asked Ross.

'No, Brighouse.'

Hope tried not to burst out laughing. 'Well, that's all good, sir,' said Hope, 'but I was wondering if you could talk to me about your sister. You say you haven't seen her, been anywhere near her. You know where she lives?'

'I don't actually know where she lives. I'm sure you do; after all, you were investigating. I left the family some time ago. They're not really up at my level. Not very intellectual, Sandra. Well, Sandra was a mess, a bit of a slut at school if you ask me; it's not good when guys are talking about how they've gone

39

after your sister. But that was Sandra. Sandra just wanted the boys and to be the girl at the centre of attention. Look where it's got her. Nathan. Oh, Nathan was "Mr-Get-your-exams"; now works in a crappy government department. And Audrey. Audrey's a cleaner. I left them behind a long time ago. I wouldn't go near any of them. You see, I've raised myself to a level of magnificence. I've raised myself to a greater standard. I've read and understood things that others don't. You do realise there is magic.'

'Illusion,' said Ross. 'You've become a great illusionist.'

'How dare you! There is no illusion.'

'You're using a dummy.'

'There is no illusion. This is rehearsal of the trappings. This is not rehearsal of the actual act. You need to understand that this is me perfecting my crowd management, my engagement with my audience. The other side I can do, and I can do well. I understand those books of mysticism. I understand. Come watch, take a look.'

The man held up a knife and pointed over to a large wheel that was spinning around. 'I can throw this with a blindfold on; blindfold me, Constable, blindfold me.'

Hope gave a nod, and Ross blindfolded the man and then grabbed his shoulders.

'What are you doing?' he said.

'I'm pointing you towards the target,' said Ross. 'I don't want you throwing it at me.'

'If I throw it, I see no problem,' said the man. 'Behold the knife.'

He held up a thin blade, which had handles coming out from it that bent at right angles before ending in a curl, protecting the hand that was holding the knife. Beside Ross's head, he began to spin the knife round and round on his hand, causing Ross to gulp.

'You see, Constable, it's not a problem. I am aware of where you are. I don't see, but I am aware.'

'Bollocks,' said Hope. 'It's not a blindfold at all.'

The man grunted, tore off the blindfold and threw it to Hope. 'You look through it.'

Hope took it. Sure enough, she couldn't see through it at all.

'Now reattach it.'

She tied it around over his eyes again and the man turned, throwing the first knife into the middle of the circle. His hands reached for a table beside him and seven knives were thrown into the large disc. He whipped off the blindfold. Hands outstretched.

'You have seen the magnificence of the Grand Master of Magic.'

'Very good,' said Hope. 'I want to clarify; have you been near anyone of your family recently?'

No,' he said.

'Have you been to any nightclubs recently?'

'Night clubs? How dare you. I wouldn't sully myself in a nightclub.'

'Let us know if you're going to leave the area,' said Hope, taking out a card. 'We have a concern for your safety regarding your sister; we're not quite sure about why she was targeted; you may become a target as well.'

'I don't have a child, and I'm a man,' he said. Which was completely obvious to Hope; she just wanted a reason for him to call her if he was leaving the area.

'Not all connections are obvious, sir,' said Hope. 'Please just do that for me.'

'If I must,' he said. 'Now, can I get back to my rehearsals?

'By all means,' said Hope. 'Come on, Constable, let's go.' The pair walked out of the hall, listening to the practised spiel of the Grand Master of Magic. Hope shook her hair, the red ponytail lagging behind her.

'Quite something, isn't he?' said Ross.

'Indeed,' said Hope, making her way across the car park. 'We were a little unexpected? Says he hasn't been near her sister, doesn't like her, doesn't like any of the other siblings. He does an act which was impressive. How he got that blindfold to be thick and I wasn't able to see through it and clearly, he was.'

'So, you don't think we saw or got anything from here?'

'I don't see much,' said Hope.

'I do,' said Ross. 'I see a man that could use a knife with precision. I see a man with an interest in mystical and occultic things. I think we gained a lot.' Ross walked over to the car and opened the door and stepped inside.

That wasn't like him, thought Hope. *Not like him. He would always tease his superior around to the idea. Let it come from them as if they've done it, not a short condescension embarrassing them. He was right, of course. That's what they had picked up. The Alan Ross she knew wouldn't have done that. It was getting to him. The anger was building; she couldn't let it build too far or a peaceful man like Alan Ross could get destroyed by that.*

Chapter 6

'Are you sure about this?' asked Macleod, staring intently at Clarissa. She nodded. 'You're convinced this is genuine? Where did you say you got the source from again?'

'One of the boys who I used to work with back in the arts section. He got in contact with a dealer he knows. Says that the nephew of the Greek tends to hide out up here.'

'But why up here? It's not exactly the place with the greatest links.'

It had taken the pair of them the best part of half a day to drive there, stuck as it was on one of those little offshoots that west of Glasgow was famous for. It was almost like the land had fingers stretching out towards the sea, stray little bits that were left dangling. Around them was barren, but in a fantastically Scottish way. Large amounts of grass, the mountains in the distance, cold sea close by, and here was a hovel.

That was the best way Macleod could describe it. Was it a house? Well, it was one of the older types built back in the day when solid corners and roofs were not the order. Instead, it almost looked like it had shrunk in on itself. It was hunched up as if protecting itself from the cold and the weather, almost as if it needed Clarissa's shawl thrown around it just to keep it from collapsing in on itself.

'It's where he goes when the heat's on. From what I'm hearing, there's a lot of chatter about these knives. It's on the quiet though. Nothing public. As if everyone's aware of the bigger picture. You don't want to get associated with something like this. If these knives are linked to the kids, linked in to murders of children, you'd be shunned by our industry, even the darker sides of it.'

Clarissa stepped out of the green car she'd parked a short distance away and wandered up with her shawl wrapped around her. She came back several times to Macleod, but the paper had gone up and he was working on that damned puzzle again.

On the drive down, he hadn't been chatty. Not that Seoras was that sort of man. Normally, he would say a few things even if it was just talking over the case. Instead, that piece of paper was out in front of him. He'd make the occasional mark on it, write the occasional letter down, and he'd mumble to himself. She asked if she could help but got told to shush.

He wasn't himself at the moment, Clarissa felt. He was struggling. Here they were scrambling around in the dark, chasing up leads but not able to do them efficiently. She never would have dreamed of walking in like this without some backup around the corner. She couldn't take Macleod in; his face was too well-known. She had her art cover. It was to a large degree intact, although she hadn't been working it recently.

Clarissa almost cursed as she stepped along the rugged path up towards the hovel of a house, her feet stepping in a large puddle. She looked at the leather boots she wore, nearly cursed again. The right foot had slid off a rock. It was small, but enough to turn her heel slightly. She winced at the pain.

That was the other thing. It wasn't like she was going to be able to run away. Whatever went on in here, she'd have to hold her bearing, have to command the situation.

Clarissa approached the wooden door that had seen better days. Paint had flaked off, but it looked intact. She thundered on it with her right hand. When no one answered, she took a step back and tried to peer in through the windows. There was no one there despite the fact there was a cosy sitting room. She saw there was a fire on, so somebody was in.

Clarissa walked round to the rear of the house where she peered in again at the same room but this time from the rear window. That fire was definitely on. She walked past the rear door, tried to see into the other room, but there was a curtain in the way. She worked out the floorplan, realising that as she had approached the house, the left-hand side was one long room with a fire. There were two rooms at least on the right-hand side. There was no height to the house beyond the ground floor. A tiny hovel, a little hideaway hole.

She walked back to the rear window of the room with the fire, and peered in. Somebody was here. She saw one, no, two cups of coffee. There were some magazines on the side.

She recognised the bare flesh across the inside of one of them. Happy material, she used to call it. For people stuck out on their own just to keep them happy. Oh, she thought, with the internet, that sort of thing was outdated these days. Maybe there wasn't internet here.

She glanced down at her phone and saw she was struggling for a signal. She placed it back inside the pocket of her trousers and peered back into the room. She heard the click too late.

Somebody grabbed her by the shoulders, hauling her backwards, and she winced as the right foot slapped down on the heel of the boot. They didn't stop dragging her and pulled her inside the door. She was hauled past a man who shut it quickly. From what she could gather at the pace she was moving, he was small but well-built.

She was dragged through into a small bedroom and tossed unceremoniously onto the bed. Someone grabbed her hair, holding her down while her hands were whipped round behind her, tied up tight.

'What the hell?' she said. 'Where's the Greek? I've come looking for the Greek.'

'Shut it.'

She felt herself being pulled up by the hair so she sat on the bed. She was able to glare into the eyes of her attacker, but they were cold, almost emotionless. The side of his face had a large scar on it and she reckoned that jaw had been broken once or twice. *Standard heavy*, she thought. He really was a heavy. The man still had his hands on her hair, her neck straining as she was pulled back. She saw the goon was dressed in black, as was a smaller man who now entered, but they both appeared to be waiting for someone.

The bed she was on was pink, a light cover on it and the curtains that prevented her from seeing out were also pink. If this was a hideaway, the cover was good because she hadn't seen any cars around either. They must have stored theirs somewhere not far away.

A figure now appeared in the doorway. The man was small, slender, early twenties at best, and had a rather girlish look to him, Clarissa thought. He wore tight leather trousers with a black jumper on top. A goatee was neatly trimmed at the bottom of his face, and his hair was cropped back short.

'You,' he said, 'you of all people.'

'Me?' asked Clarissa. 'Do I know you?'

'No, but my uncle did. My uncle got run over because of you. My uncle's dead because of you. You set him up.'

'I did not set him up. I came looking for some knives to buy,' she said, and found her arm twisted up behind her back.

'Stop lying. Show her what we do to liars.' Clarissa wondered what was coming next, then felt her arm driven up impossibly high, right across the back, and she yelled out in pain.

'Now, tell me the truth. What happened to my uncle? Why did you set him up? What is it you want?'

'I want the knives,' said Clarissa. 'I've just come to purchase knives.'

'There are no knives for purchase,' said the man, 'and you're not going to tell anybody about this place. You can cut her,' he said quietly to the small man.

Clarissa tried to force her way out, tried to break the hold she was in. As she watched, the small man took a butterfly knife out from his pocket, then clicked the button, making the blade whip round until it resembled a full knife.

'Not here though,' he said. 'Not here. We need to do it outside, wash the blood down easier. Around the back; nobody will see,' he said.

Clarissa was hauled up onto her feet by the hair, her right ankle screaming at her as the man basically dragged her by the arm and the hair out of the door to the rear of the building. He pushed her up against the wall and delivered a punch to her stomach, causing her to buckle over, and then to throw up. Her feet went from under and she collapsed to the ground only to find her hair being pulled back up.

Her leg slid out, struggling to find purchase on the vomit she'd put on the ground. The small man then came up to her with the knife. She was being held by the larger of the two, pressed tight against the wall, a hand on her throat half choking her as the little guy waved the knife in front of her face.

'Where first, love? That skin's had a bit of use, hasn't it? Old bird, aye? Old bird with a bit of money. You're something else, tell me. Cut all sorts, I have. Cut all sorts. I know your kind. Yes. I'll do a bit of the skin here and there. I might start with the knees, start cutting a bit in there. Should be able to leave enough weight on them so it will hurt, then you can scream here. Nobody'll hear you here.'

Clarissa let out an almighty scream, hoping Macleod could hear her. The car was further down and couldn't be seen where they parked it. She wondered could he even hear.

'Ha, scream away, girlie, because they won't hear anything. No one will hear you. Now, let's see.'

The man reached in under her shawl and found the belt of her trousers. He barely undid it, and pulled the trousers down, leaving her in complete dishevelment, and bent down to her knee.

'Sometimes we take the blade just in here behind the kneecap,' he said. 'Oh, that'll hurt. That'll hurt.' Clarissa looked away. She didn't want to see what he was doing.

A shadow appeared around the edge of the house, and a metal bar whipped past Clarissa's face into the big man who was standing there. It caught him smack on the nose, blood spurted everywhere, and he cried out, reaching up. Before the man with the knife down below could react, the metal bar was taken down onto his head, and a third blow was then swung at the man who had ordered the torture. He ricocheted off the wall, falling to the ground holding his head, blood seeping from the side.

The dark figure wasn't finished, however. He took the long metal pole he had and drove it into the stomach of the large man, before following that up with a crackdown on the knees of the small figure who then dropped the knife. The three men rolled in agony before the larger man was hit again on the head and seemed to pass out.

Clarissa, freed of all encumberment, held her back against the wall and reached down for her trousers, pulling them up and doing the belt as quick as she could. She then stepped forward, lifting the knife away from the small man and giving him a large kick right into the centre of his stomach. He doubled up.

She winched, feeling the pain that had gone through her ankle in delivering it. She looked up at Macleod, a hoodie over his face, the balaclava he'd worn previously so that only his eyes could be seen, the large raincoat and a set of gloves on.

'You,' said Clarissa, marching over to the boss. He didn't have long enough hair to pull him up by, so she simply grabbed the black outfit he was wearing and pulled him close to her face. 'What happened to the knives? Where did they go?'

'I'm not telling you,' he said. 'I'm not telling you.'

'They killed kids with them. They damn well killed kids with them,' said Clarissa. 'You tell me, or I'll gut you.'

She almost expected Seoras behind her to flinch, to say something, to say no, but he stood resolutely, holding the metal bar which had a small amount of blood dripping off one end.

49

'It wasn't me. I just did part of it. It wasn't me. God's sake, don't kill me.'

'Depends on what you tell me.'

'My life won't be worth living if I tell you.'

'You tell me, you've got a chance,' said Clarissa. 'If you don't tell me, you haven't got any. Now tell me. Where the hell are those knives?'

'I was picked up to run them, okay? Picked up to run them. The people who picked them, you don't squeal on. You don't squeal on these people.'

The metal bar was beside the man's face, pushing his cheek. 'Like I said, it's up to you.' Clarissa grinned in the man's face with an almost maniacal look.

'Okay. The McGoverns. All right? The McGoverns—they did it.'

Clarissa went to ask about the McGoverns, but before she spoke, a hand went on her shoulder. Macleod thumbed that they should leave, and Clarissa slapped the man with the back of her hand.

'You ever touch me like that again,' she said, 'and you won't walk.' She spat in his face. 'You can tell them Queenie was here,' and with that, the pair of them disappeared off back towards the car. On the way, Macleod threw the metal pipe off the side of the road.

As soon as they entered the car, Clarissa put the foot down and they drove quickly away, realising that nobody had got round to the front of the house by the time they'd passed it.

'That was a bit . . .'

'Reckless,' said Macleod. 'That was reckless.'

'Sorry, but we need to . . .'

'We need to find it. I get it. We need to chase this trail, but you could have been killed if I hadn't stepped in.'

'Thank you,' she said; 'you really had to.'

Macleod was looking out the window. 'Yes,' he said, 'I really had to. You know what the worst of it is? It felt good. It actually felt good. Somebody did something to those kids and these guys all had a hand in it. This isn't good,' he said. 'There's no limits on me. There's nothing to stop me. If we hadn't needed information, I might have . . . well.'

Clarissa reached over with one hand, keeping the other on the wheel. She tapped his knee.

'You saved me and yes, you gave them a beating, but they were about to kill me. They were about to do a lot of things. I think it's okay.'

Macleod shook his head.

He remained silent as she drove back towards Glasgow. After ten minutes, she thought she could venture a question.

'He said the McGoverns. Do you know them?'

Macleod nodded slowly. 'I know them. And this time, I'll go see them.'

'So, you've run into them before?'

'Oh yes,' said Macleod, 'and they don't like me. I put half of them in jail.'

Chapter 7

Hope drove the car up to the rather bland building of the Department of Work and Pensions in Inverness. Together with Ross, she marched into the front reception area to find out that Nathan Mackie, the brother of Sandra and Kyle Mackie, was currently on leave. He'd been a model employee for many years, according to the boss, and he currently should be at home as he hadn't told anyone he was going on any foreign holiday or a trip. Hope took an address. It tallied up with one that Ross already had, and together, they drove towards the centre of Inverness and eventually to a small flat along a rather crowded street.

Hope stood banging on the door, but no one replied from inside. The flat on the ground floor had mostly covered-up windows, curtains drawn across, so seeing in was awkward. Ross looked at one window and thought he could peer in and began to take photographs, saying it was easier for the camera to pick up the image, which he could then look at. Hope didn't want to stop him, so instead walked to the next door along to the neighbouring flat and banged on it. The door opened to a young man who Hope reckoned could only be about nineteen or twenty. He glanced up at her, smiling broadly.

'Hi. Is something wrong? Can I help you?'

His face said that he desperately did want to help her, but Hope pulled out the warrant card and held it up to the man. 'Hi, there. I'm DS Hope McGrath and my colleague over there's DC Ross. We were hoping to talk to your neighbour. I believe it's a Nathan Mackie.'

'Oh, yes, Nathan. He's not in at the moment.'

'Kind of worked that out,' said Hope. 'Do you know where he is?'

'No, I think he went out with his dog earlier on.'

'Okay,' said Hope. 'Do you know what sort of a person he is?' She became aware that the man was staring up and down at her.

'Are you okay?' she asked.

'I'm fine,' he said. 'You're very tall.'

'I am,' said Hope, 'and I'm aware of that.'

'Do you want to come in?' the man said.

'Right. I can do if you want,' said Hope, 'but I'm very happy to talk out here. If we come in, then DC Ross will have to join us.'

'Okay,' the man said. Again, he was watching her very intently. She looked over her shoulder and shouted, 'Ross, come inside here a minute, please.'

'Just getting a couple more photographs. I'll be in in a second.'

Hope nodded and followed the man in front of her into a small kitchen area where he showed her to a stool.

'What sort of coffee do you like?' he asked. 'Do you know coffee's very, very unique? I like coffee.'

'My boss likes coffee as well. I'm happy to take whatever coffee you want.' The man walked up to her, close to her face, looked in her eyes. Then he gave a sniff.

'Kenyan. Kenyan Blue Mountain. That'll suit you. It's classy but it's got a little bit of kick.'

Hope almost burst out laughing, but the man's face was deadly serious.

'Do you mind if I ask if you're working currently?'

The man gave a nod and a proud smile. 'I do computers. I do programming. I get the bus down and then I go in and they give me the programming to do. I do it and then I come back, and it gives me all of this.'

The voice was almost simplistic. 'Do you have a lot of friends?' asked Hope.

'I have friends at the programming and friends at the groups I go to.'

'Where's that?'

'I go to St. Thomas's tonight. We all go out. You have some drinks. Ann'll be there. I like Ann.'

'Right,' said Hope. The man came over to her, leaning in, his shoulders touching with her, and he gave her a broad smile. 'Never had a police officer in here before. I think I recognise you.'

'From where?' asked Hope.

'You've been on the telly. Hope McGrath, Hope McGrath. You always wear your hair up like that. You have that leather jacket. It's always a leather jacket. You work for Macleod. That's Alan Ross out there and you have a Clarissa Urquhart, too. I found their names out. It wasn't difficult. They mentioned them in an article, but you and Macleod are always on the telly. You're my first police officer in here.'

Hope smiled and realised she was dealing with a challenged individual, a vulnerable adult as they would say.

'Can you tell me about Nathan, please?' asked Hope. 'I just want to find out a few things about him.'

'He don't talk to me much,' said the man. 'Doesn't talk to me much at all. I think he thinks I'm strange. Nathan wouldn't let you give him a hug. Do you let people give you a hug?'

'Not normally when I'm working,' said Hope. 'The people I tend to deal with don't generally react to hugs.'

The man smiled. 'I like hugs. I think you would hug people.'

Alan Ross walked in to see the man up close to Hope, touching shoulders and smiling, almost inches from her face. He gave a little cough.

'This is DC Ross. Alan, my partner. Alan, this is . . . oh, I haven't even asked your name, have I?'

'John Oswald. John Oswald Bishop.'

'Nice to meet you, Mr Bishop,' said Ross.

'John Oswald. Call me John Oswald. I'll call you Alan. I've seen you on the telly.'

'Right,' said Ross.

Hope put a hand up. 'I was asking John Oswald if he knew anything about Nathan next door. You were going to tell me, John.'

John wasn't listening and had beetled over to Ross, going up close to him and then sniffing.

'He wouldn't like Kenyan. He would be more Colombian.'

The man beetled off, taking out a separate tub of coffee. Hope realised that they were each being made the coffee he had talked about. They waited five minutes until the man put coffees in front of the pair of them and joined them, sitting up on a high chair so close to Hope that their knees touched.

'What can you tell me about next door?'

'Well,' said John Oswald, 'the thing is that he's a bit like me, on his own a lot. He has the dog, but the dog's . . . well, I don't like the dog. It barks at me. It shouts and gets on at me. He takes it out for walks quite a bit, but he's been gone quite long today. Went out this morning.'

'Is there anything unusual happens at his house?' asked Ross.

'Unusual? I don't know. I don't go in. He doesn't let me in. He's not a man who would give you a hug.'

'Does anybody else go in?' asked Hope.

'Mrs Lam. Mrs Lam's the cleaner. He has a cleaner, Mrs Lam. She talks to me sometimes. She's a nice woman. Then there's some other men that go in, but they don't come on their own. One man came on his own, but lots of men don't come on their own. They all come together. He has a flat like me so it's too many people. I wouldn't let that many people into this flat. Can you imagine? It's nice here. Look, you and me and Alan, it's all very cosy and we have the coffee, but a large group like that, they'd be sitting on the floor, lots of them.'

'How often did they go in?'

'Two, three, four times in a year, but I remember them all. Well, I remember, not them because they come in and their faces are covered.'

'With hoods and that?' asked Ross.

The man snorted and gave out a laugh. 'Hoods and things. That's crazy. No, they have caps pulled down over their face. Caps and hats and things. I look out the window and I never see their face. They're different sizes. Some big, some small, but I think they're all men. Although . . .'

'What?' asked Hope.

'One of them, I think it was a woman because when you look down, you see, I couldn't see the top half, but when you look down, she had those . . . well, you know.' The man smiled at

Hope.

'What?'

'Had that leggings on that you women like. I think it was a woman's bottom.' He almost sniggered.

'Okay, so how many went in?' asked Ross.

The man looked over quickly at Ross and Hope tapped him on the shoulder. 'Alan's just asking a question. It's okay. How many?'

John Oswald screwed his face up and then twisted his neck and moved this way and that for a bit and then he stopped. 'Twelve.'

'You sure?' asked Hope.

'Twelve. Very sure.'

'Twelve went in?' asked Ross. 'Or twelve, including Nathan?'

Bang on, thought Hope. *Me asking the questions, trying to be clever and Ross simply clarifies it, gets to the core of it. I wouldn't have thought of saying that.*

'Twelve, including him,' said John Oswald.

'Excellent,' said Hope. 'But you don't recognise any of them except you think one's a woman?'

'That's right,' said John Oswald and then sniggered again, 'because there was a woman's bottom.'

Hope gave a little laugh and encouragement. 'Where do you think he's gone with his dog?'

'He goes to the park normally. I've seen him a few times.' The man looked a little bit anxious.

'When you say you've seen him a few times, what do you mean?' asked Hope. 'Did you try to see him?'

'I just was there,' he said.

'Did you follow him?' asked Ross.

The young man went quite shy, turning away from Hope.

She placed her hand on his shoulder. 'It's okay; we're not here to arrest you or anything. We just want to know how you know.'

The man turned around and smiled at Hope. 'I followed him. I tracked him one day. I always wondered where he went.'

'He didn't see you?' asked Ross.

'No,' said the man. 'I'm clever. I'm very clever. People think I'm stupid, think I'm simple. I'm not simple. I might struggle with some things.' He looked up and smiled at Hope. 'Not good personally is what they say, especially with women.'

'Okay,' said Hope. 'We all have our problems but you're not daft, are you? You were able to follow him without him seeing.'

'Yes, and he went round the park. Round and round the park and he picked up the poo from his dog. He has those green plastic bags, and he puts it into the bin that's on the far northern side of the park. He doesn't use the poop bin on the west.'

The man's level of detail was amazing. They continued the conversation until Hope realised they weren't finding anything more out and decided she should go look for Nathan in the park.

'Don't tell him we were here,' said Hope. 'We'll find him ourselves.'

'I won't,' said the man.

As they got to the front door, Hope turned around to thank him. 'Thank you,' she said, extending a hand, and the man reached forward and grabbed it. Then, without warning, he flung himself forward wrapping an arm around her and placing his head just under Hope's chin. He cuddled her tight before Ross reached over and went, 'Hey.'

'It's okay,' said Hope, 'but that's enough, John Oswald.'

The man stepped back, blushing. 'Sorry,' he said.

'You hug good and I'm going to go now,' said Hope. 'Thank you, but don't hug women like that unless they ask.' The man nodded.

With the door closed behind them, Hope looked over at Ross who produced his phone and started showing some pictures to Hope.

'Most of the rooms are normal from what I can see looking through one of the curtains. It's hard to see but if I blow it up like this, look.'

Hope peered through the rather murky picture, but it was clear there were several upside-down crosses on the wall. There were other images that looked like mutilation. However, it could have been the inside of a teenager's room with some weird posters. Having pictures and symbols weren't against the law. The pictures were produced using pencil and paint; they weren't live ones.

'I think we need to have a serious chat with Nathan. It's an awful strong occultic connection,' said Hope. 'I'm wondering if the upside-down cross out of the symbols carved on the kids was the dominant one and the rest of it, well, maybe that's just cover.'

Chapter 8

Clarissa watched Macleod sitting on the bench with a large paper out in front of him, a coffee and a chicken sandwich on his side. The sandwich hadn't been touched; the coffee barely sipped. They'd been driving back towards Glasgow when Macleod had told her to pull the car over. The paper had been in front of him again. He had been scrawling letters all over it and amongst all the symbols and the signs.

What was strange about him was the fact he was sitting with the hood up. Macleod had never worn a hoodie in his life until this recent escapade with Clarissa, and it was almost like he was enjoying it. Some bizarre, nigh old-age teenager huddled up, focused deeply on the paper in front of him. She found it hard to sit and watch, for her own coffee had gone some time ago. The wrap, for let's face it, wraps were much classier than sandwiches, had been dispatched as well, and now Clarissa was frustrated.

The packet of crisps had gone too. Macleod had refused one, and then she sat on the bonnet of the little green sports car. She wanted to know what he was doing. Her ankle was still sore. Her hair, however, was looking much better because she'd taken the time to brush it while Macleod was working on his paper. Her nerves, though, were somewhat shattered because that had been close, far too close.

He'd given her a row for it. Maybe she had been reckless, but there were lives at risk here. She was over the threshold, having to go beyond where she'd gone before because they were working in the dark, working away from the main group. Sure, Ross and Hope had been helpful, but they still were locked in under the normal police rules. Macleod never would've struck somebody the way he did there. He must have realised her life was under threat. Normally, he would announce 'Police', but then he wasn't operating in that capacity and they were out on their own, two old farts at the end of the day. *That's what they were. Two daft, old farts*, thought Clarissa, *taking on the world and our best long behind us*.

The sound of a paper being folded up caused Clarissa to look over and see Macleod take to his feet. She waited, expecting him to walk back towards the car, maybe even announce what he'd found out, but instead, he started striding over to the sea. The bench where he had been sitting had a small path in front of it and behind it, the waves were crashing in on what was a blustery day. There was a small amount of beach before you reached them, and then wet sand, and she saw Macleod stride over directly to this part of the beach. He bent down, picking up a loose stick before standing, back to the waves, looking down at blank sand.

Clarissa shook her head. *What on earth? Here we go*. She limped over towards him; as she got down onto the sand, his hand shot out.

'Back. Leave the space.'

'You're freaking me out now, Seoras.'

61

'Just stay back. Or if you want to come around and look at it this way, stand behind me.'

That was it. There was no pardon, excuse me, no explanation of what he was about to do, so Clarissa took him at his word, gave him a wide berth until she'd walked up behind him and stood looking at the blank sand.

He reached into his pocket and took out the paper he'd been working on previously. After giving it a glance, it returned to his pocket and Macleod started drawing in the sand. Clarissa recognised some symbols. She'd seen them on the paper.

Slowly, Macleod drew, until there on the sand spread out in a vast tableau before him were all the symbols that the paper contained. Then he drew the letter E, not once, not twice, but three times underneath different symbols. Then A was written, then there was an O, a T, then a V. He continued this, stopping every now and again, thinking, watching closely, and then examining the paper again until at last, there was an English alphabet letter underneath each symbol. He stepped back quietly, not saying anything but staring at the sand.

'Tides coming in, Seoras. I hate to tell you this, but what you've just written is going to be gone in an hour.'

'Get your camera out; photograph it.'

Clarissa took out her phone, tried to adjust until she could see everything and realised she was struggling to get all the letters in, so she scurried round to the top of the diagram Macleod had drawn where she had more height and was able to see much clearer everything that had been written. She snapped about four photographs, checked them on the phone that she could actually read each one, blowing up the picture, and then returned to Macleod again, giving his drawing a wide birth.

'What's this?'

'It's the code,' said Macleod. 'It's the code of the letter.'

'But how does that work?' she asked. 'Some of those symbols, two or three are of the same letter.'

'Yes,' he said. 'It's quite clever, isn't it? You overdo the number of symbols. There's not a one-to-one match. There's more than that, so we have two E's together or two T's. It doesn't look like it.'

Clarissa stared. 'So, you're telling me that you know what the letter says?'

'Yes,' said Macleod, 'I do, but I want to check it.'

He pulled out the paper in front of him and stood, going back and forward from one to the other, and then he stepped forward in the sand, rubbed out a few letters and wrote more letters back where the sand had been disturbed. He stepped back again and looked once more.

'Something's not here,' he said out loud.

'Well, you got me,' said Clarissa, to which she received a waved hand telling her to shush.

All of a sudden, Macleod turned and began walking down the beach. Clarissa went to follow him, but he told her to stop, protect what he'd written. Again, she looked at him but did as bidden and watched as he continued down the beach. He stepped here and there, then found a small stone and skimmed it into the sea. He picked up another, this time making it bounce three times before it disappeared into the water, and then he picked up a third. As he drew his arm back, he let the stone drop and strode deliberately back up to Clarissa.

'Good, you've come back. Now can we . . .'

'Shut it. Just shut up, woman,' he said. 'Just shut up.'

Clarissa reared for a moment and stepped aside and watched

as he raced from one symbol to the other, changing about six different letters. He then resumed his previous position with the piece of paper and his head scanning back and forward, back and forward, and then he turned to her with a grin on his face.

'What?' she asked. 'What's up?'

He held up the paper in front of her. 'This,' said Macleod. 'This here, this is a kill order. Winston has been ordered to kill the man who shamed the group.'

'Where?' asked Clarissa.

'I don't know,' replied Macleod. 'It doesn't say that. It just says to kill him.'

'Who is the other man? I take it is a man.'

'Well, it says to kill a brother, so I'm assuming it's a man,' said Macleod, 'but doesn't say who he is.'

'Okay,' said Clarissa. 'So, you're telling me that you've stood here, worked all this out, and the only thing that letter tells us is that Winston is off to kill somebody who apparently did a botched job, so we reckon this could be the person who killed Sandra Mackie's child?'

'Yes,' said Macleod, 'but we don't know who that is.'

'Okay,' said Clarissa. 'So now we know that Winston is off to kill somebody who we don't know and we don't know where they live or we don't know where Winston is going and we can't put a shout-out amongst the force to find him before he does it because you and I are not meant to even have been in there.'

'That's pretty much the long and short of it,' said Macleod.

'Great. Well, that was worth stopping for.'

'Enough,' said Macleod, 'enough. I've just broke a code that was . . . well, it took a lot.'

64

He marched over and sat down on the bench. Clarissa wondered what was up with the man. She followed him, sat down, and waited for him to speak. After five minutes when he hadn't, she tapped him on his shoulder.

'This is the bit where you pour your feelings out, you know. This is the bit where you say, Clarissa, this is how I am feeling, this is why I'm in this particular mood at the moment. This is getting to me because . . .'

'No, it isn't,' said Macleod.

'I think it is,' said Clarissa. 'I'm not carrying on this jaunt until you tell me what the heck's going on up in that head.'

'No,' said Macleod. 'There's only two people that get to hear those things. Jane gets to hear everything, and listen, when it's not to do with the work. I share very little about the work with her. I share about me, not about her. I share maybe management stuff, but I never share with her the bits about the actual case. You don't share the bit about the children, about what you see. You don't share the horror.'

'So, who gets that then?' asked Clarissa. 'Who do you chat that to, God?'

'No,' said Macleod, and gave a half smile. 'She wouldn't thank you for calling her God, although she's quite tall.'

Clarissa nodded. She knew who it was. 'Is that where the grumpiness is coming from? You can talk it over with me.'

'I haven't known you that long,' said Macleod. 'You're a good copper, you're dogged, you're ready to fight, but I couldn't let you see that scene the second time, not after the first. You're not good at that bit. Well, no one is good at that bit, but you're not in a place to help somebody else talk that over, to talk about the fear of not getting to the bottom of this, about seeing the next body, the next wee one. These are wee ones,' said

Macleod, 'wee ones. How do you do that to wee ones?'

'I don't know,' said Clarissa, turning away, tears in her eyes. 'I don't know. I don't know, Seoras. All I know is we're going to get the bastards because you don't do this; this is sick. That's why I'm here. That's why I'm not resting my foot up and trust me, I think it's getting worse by the hour.'

'Hope, I can talk to about this. You never really understood, did you; neither does Ross, why we get on so well? Why it is Hope and I work well as a team.'

'Not really, no. Why is it? Enlighten me,' she said, smiling as a tear rolled down her cheek.

'Ross never questions me, or very rarely. You question everything—you chin me. Not question—you chin me. You poke fun, which is fine. It's good for the others to see me like that at times. But Hope—Hope is as loyal as they come, doggedly loyal. If they call you my Rottweiler, she's my Labrador but she's also my confidant. I never show worry, I don't show much stress, I don't show anger, but right now, I could snap the necks of those people. When I hit them with that iron bar back when you were in trouble, part of me wanted to pummel them, sending these knives across, these knives that went into the kids.'

'You're only human, Seoras. Give yourself a break; you're only human.'

'I'm meant to be more than that, don't you understand that? This thing you see, you all see church, you see symbols, you see propriety, you see a piousness in the church. It's not what it's about, it's about being the better person, being a better person. This thing, this sickness that takes me down to their level, I just want to get the world rid of them, I want to rip them apart, I want to destroy them. It's not the message, is it? It's not His

66

message.'

Clarissa reached over and put her arm around his shoulder. 'I really don't know what to say. I've not been much of a religious person.'

Macleod laughed. 'It's got to be the truest thing you've ever said to me.'

'Fair enough,' she said. 'But I'll promise you this; we'll get these bastards and we'll stop them.'

He took her arm off him and turned and stared seriously at her, breathing heavily. 'That's it, Clarissa, do you understand? That's where I can't be because I will go for them. I will tear them apart if I focus on that. That's what the job gives me. The method, the strength to follow the order, because that's what we are, law and order. We're not the barbarians killing that which we don't like.' He stood up and walked back to the car and she shook her head.

'Maybe sometimes we should be,' she said. 'Maybe sometimes.' She felt an eerie chill as she stood up, for her boss never spoke like this.

Chapter 9

Hope stared out amongst the parkland, looking for a Labrador dog and the face of Nathan Mackie. The photograph was an old one, pulled from a DWP pass that Mackie last renewed over four years ago. As for the Labrador, it had come from a description by John Oswald. They had scanned the park, walked from end to end, and across, but still hadn't seen him. They were just about to meet up in the middle again when Hope felt her phone vibrating in her pocket. She took it out, saw Clarissa's face looking back at her and pressed the accept button.

'What's happening your end?' asked Hope. 'Are things going well?'

'If you're asking about the foot, no. If you're asking how the other things going, that's making some headway. We've been to the bookshop and the book owner wasn't there, but we were able to find out something about him. Apparently, he's got instructions to go and see one of the other group. Close the guy's account.'

Hope stopped in her tracks. 'Say again?'

'He's going to have to close the account of one of the rest of his group, the bookshop owner will.'

'How did we know this?'

'There was a message left at the bookshop. When we got there, the bookshop owner wasn't about. There was a message left but their handwriting was very difficult. I've just had an old man break it down for me.'

Hope would have laughed at that description, but she was much more interested in what was being said.

'Just let me get hold of this for a moment,' she said. 'Hold up. You've gone to the bookshop; the bookshop owner wasn't there. However, there was a message left. The message wasn't easy to read. You had to get an old guy to look at the handwriting. The old guy's come up and said that the bookshop owner has got to go and close the account of someone else, who belonged to the group that has to do with the bookshop owner?'

'That's basically it,' said Clarissa. 'Sounds like a proper closing. Terminal! No way back into the group.'

'How's that old man doing then?' asked Hope.

'He's holding up. We're both holding up. I think this is big time. We've also been tracing where the implements were. We took a look where my package had disappeared to.'

The code wasn't very subtle, thought Hope. *If anybody actually listened to this, surely they'd work out what they were on about.* She guessed it was all about plausible denial. They'd make up some hocus pocus about what was going on.

Frankly, Hope was beginning to care less. Things seem to be moving. It was getting to that point where she knew Macleod would make a move; Macleod would stretch out, would see what was happening, and go for it.

Something was coming to her. *Was one of the Mackie brothers the problem? Nathan Mackie had just disappeared; he wasn't in the park. There'd been a shame on the group. Well, the Mackie brothers were part of the group possibly*, she thought. *If it's a shame on the group it will be about Sandra Mackie and there was someone involved there. Someone who had slept with her. Someone who couldn't be identified from DNA. It had to be, didn't it?*

It was still a hunch but was it a plausible lead that she was looking at. Somebody's life was in danger though. She couldn't hold back. She couldn't wait for proof. She couldn't wait for evidence. That would simply arrive in the form of a dead man.

Just now, she wished Macleod was with her. They could talk. They could look at it, evaluate the risk, and go. In her head came the message from Lawson. 'You should be the DI. You should put forward for it.' *Well, these were the decisions she'd have to make, to live with. Weren't they?*

'I'm going to have to talk to upstairs to help. This is too far. I think I know whose account is getting closed down.'

'What?' asked Clarissa. 'How on earth?'

'Let's just say a possible match came up on the DNA. I'm going to talk to upstairs.'

'Okay, if you think you should bring them in, but it's still very dodgy ground.'

Hope realised they were talking off the code. That didn't really seem to matter now, not when this much was at stake.

'I've got two possible people that could be. Tell Macleod when you don't have DNA, or you don't have significantly different DNA with regards to testing, it has to come from the same line, siblings. Jona said siblings, Clarissa. We've been to see both male siblings. I need to pull them both in for their safety. Find them before somebody else finds one of them.'

She heard a whispering in the background. Clarissa was clearly passing the message on to Macleod.

'The old man says yes. I don't think he's happy about it, but he says yes.'

'He also says your DCI won't go for it,' said Hope. 'There's no proof. There's just a line of thought. He says because the risk is so great, the person's life is at stake, you go and you do it anyway, even though it could knock off our possible lead. Might be better to set a trap but we don't know where to set it. That's what he says.'

'Yes,' said Clarissa, 'that's exactly what he said.'

'Where are you two off to?' asked Hope.

'Somewhere in Glasgow. We'll tell you about it when we get there. Looking up the package.'

'Good luck,' said Hope and closed the phone call quickly. She looked around. Ross had nearly reached her and she ran over to him. Quickly she passed on the information she'd been given.

'We need to do this somehow. We know where the magician is; we don't know where Nathan is. Maybe get somebody on the magician.' Her phone was back up to her ear, a number having been dialled. Soon she heard the DCI's voice on the other end.

'Alan,' said Hope. 'We've got some developments. Jona came over and was talking about the lack of DNA as we told you. So, we've gone to see both brothers. There's information coming from elsewhere. Information that says that this may be a big group and they may be about to close things down.

'Information coming from where?' asked Lawson.

'That could compromise my source. They're very wary at the moment of the police force,' lied Hope. There was no indication of that. She was trying to think of how to keep Macleod out of it.

71

'Well, that's not great, is it? They're saying what?'

'They are saying that one of these two brothers of Sandra Mackie could be the killer but the group's wanting to finish him off. It looks like Macleod might have been right with his group idea. There's more than one killer.'

'That still sounds rather fanciful. Where's the evidence for this? How do they know?'

Hope couldn't deal without bringing up what Macleod had been doing and she wasn't quite ready to throw him under the bus like that just so she could get backup—backup she wasn't sure was still going to arrive.

'I can't say on that. You got to trust me on this one, Alan. I've got a feeling in my gut about it. I want to find these two brothers. I want to bring them in. I feel they may be in trouble.'

'Well, I don't know,' said Lawson, sounding worried. 'Ian Lamb's still dead. Nobody else has died since. Seems to me we got our man. There's nothing else going on, so just to please you,' said Alan, 'you can spend the rest of the afternoon on it, but do this for me: seriously consider going for DI.'

'Thanks,' said Hope, and went to put the phone down.

'No, no, no. Hang on,' he said. 'When I say seriously go for DI, I want you to come up and talk it through with me. I've been there. I can assist you, take you through the questions and things that they'd ask you in an interview. There'll be a post coming up very, very soon. We can make a good partnership, you and me. You never know, you might even get Ross up to DS, build the department up a bit. This will really lift our kudos, building on nabbing Lamb.'

'Okay,' said Hope. 'I'll do that, but I want to run this through first. I need to get on top of this.'

'Ten a.m. tomorrow morning,' said the DCI. 'Let's start early.

I mean, there's nothing else going on. Check this out this afternoon and providing nothing big kicks off, we can spend most of tomorrow on that. You can come up to my office, sergeant. You won't be out and about. You could probably drop the hair down as well.'

Hope ignored the comment. Was the guy actually trying to flirt with her? She wasn't sure but she didn't have time to sit and mess about on the phone. 'Got to go, sir,' she said.

'Alan. It's Alan.'

'Got to go, Alan.'

'Ten tomorrow.'

That was the last she heard from the phone call because Hope closed it as Ross had arrived. 'We need to get out and search. We got the two Mackie brothers. He said we can have the afternoon on it but he's not giving us any backup. I'll keep looking for Nathan. I want you to go and start looking for Kyle. He was at the hall, find him. Sit on him, whatever.'

'Can't we call anyone in for backup?'

'We don't know where yet. If we turn around and call it in, the DCI will likely block it. If nothing happens, he'll have our guts for garters. No, when you get on top of this, if you see anything looks dodgy, you phone it in. Okay?'

'Of course,' said Ross. He went to turn away, but Hope grabbed his arm.

'No risks, Alan. No risks. We're all liable to push it too far at the moment; don't.' He nodded. 'Get underway,' she shouted after him, took out the car keys and threw them to him. 'You take it. I'm on foot from here. He's got to be about here somewhere.'

With Ross disappearing off to find Kyle Mackie, Hope continued to hunt for Nathan. Rather than just look from afar, she started stopping dog walkers, showing the picture of the man, suggesting he was with a Labrador. A young woman said he was off to the far end of the park and Hope paced up that way but found no one there had seen him. Another younger lad suggested he may have left the park heading towards the large river.

It was nearly afternoon, the winter sun was setting, and Hope was worried that she wasn't going to find him sooner rather than later. *Would Nathan Mackie have gone home? Surely by now, unless of course, he knew he was being followed.* Hope ran back, checked the flat again but found no one at home. By the time she got back to the park, it was truly dark.

She spoke to a man with a large St. Bernard. He advised that a man with a Labrador had been last seen walking towards the island at Ness River. Hope thanked him and ran all the way there. Breathing deeply, standing in her leather jacket and jeans, she felt the chill of the air coming in and wondered what she should do. If only she could take a quick walk. The islands were located out in the river, and you could chop back and forward over small bridges quickly.

She ran around and then saw a dog at the far end of one of the islands. It was a Labrador, and a man was walking with it. Surely it had to be him. Hope ran forward, the green vegetation on either side of the path, until she reached the bottom and there was no one. She looked along the riverbank. On the far side of the river was the man with the Labrador again. She took off but noticed that he was starting to run quickly now as well. As she reached the bank, he turned back to the Ness Islands, cutting across one of the other bridges.

Hope decided to spin round and come back and went across her own bridge, arriving in the dark of the middle island. It was then she heard a voice. Quickly, she knelt down and sent a text to Ross advising she'd found Nathan Mackie. She stood up, walked slowly forward but then found herself ducking out of the way as a large man came in the other direction. He was clearly looking for something and only Hope's ability to hide in behind one of the bushes meant that he hadn't seen her.

Quickly, Hope typed in another message asking Ross for assistance because there seemed to be more than herself and Nathan Mackie on the island. She heard more sounds, footsteps walking the path. After seeing who had walked past her previously, she decided she wasn't going to step out until she was ready.

Hope decided to creep through the undergrowth to see if she could find how many people were on the island. As she did so, she heard at least two other male voices. There was 'That's him. That's him.' They quickly sped off.

Hope emerged from the bushes out onto the path. She strode quickly down after the men she had heard until she heard their voices close again and ducked in back into the undergrowth. She could hear them breathing heavily, one man asking the other if he'd got him.

'He's bringing him up now,' said a voice. 'He'll be with us in a second.'

Hope stepped out from the undergrowth. There was a chance to get there to change things. As Hope stepped out from the vegetation, a hand grabbed her shoulder. She lashed out and struck someone on the chin, but something hit her on the back of the head. She dropped to her knees but swung her hand out, grabbing the ankle of a man close to her. She then drove her elbow up, catching him in between his legs causing him to buckle over. She then tried to get up to her feet but stumbled and someone hit her again on the back of the head. Everything went black.

Chapter 10

Having made his way back to the hall where Ross and Hope had initially met Kyle Mackie conducting his magic act, Ross found the place to be empty. Ross decided to return to Kyle Mackie's house where he saw the lights on inside, and after furtively moving up to the window, he saw the man sitting down and watching football. He was safe inside.

They'd already interviewed him, so Ross decided the best policy was to sit in front of the house and see if anyone would approach. If someone was out to kill him, they didn't appear at present to be inside the house, and Ross thought he might have the opportunity to catch the person in the act. Normally, he'd have someone with him to be able to run to the loo, get himself a coffee and control the stake out. He would never go hungry or get too fatigued. For now, though, he was on his own and he wasn't quite sure what would happen when it came to the end of the day.

The DCI had only given him permission to continue these investigations today. How far would he allow them to go into the next day and beyond? As Ross sat in the car just down from a streetlight, he saw a woman walking along the road, carrying a bottle of wine in her right hand. She was dressed in a smart coat, pulled up tight around her neck, and walked in a pair of high heels. Her blonde hair flowed out over the jacket, and her pace didn't diminish at all as she approached Kyle Mackie's home.

She walked up, banged on the door, and Kyle Mackie opened it to welcome her in. From Ross' position, he could see her jacket being taken off, and she wore a smart red dress underneath. Mackie seemed delighted at her arrival and certainly not surprised from what Ross could gather through his binoculars. Once the door closed, Ross continued to watch, and saw through the windows the woman appearing to kiss Mackie several times. The blinds were then pulled down. It was about an hour and a half before the downstairs lights went off and the upstairs ones went on.

Ross jumped out of the car, made a sweeping pattern around the building, making sure no one was about, and nothing was afoot. He doubted that he would see Kyle Mackie for the rest of the evening, and so he decided to sit back in the car, chill out as best he could, and wait for instructions from his boss. Part of him wanted to phone, just to have someone to talk to, and he thought he might have to ring his own partner back at home if he got too bored. It wasn't best to disturb Hope while she was in pursuit of someone. You never knew what the situation could be, and the phone call at the end of the day was utterly pointless. He had nothing to report. After all, there was nothing doing with Kyle Mackie except a progression in his love life.

Feeling the vibration of his phone, he took it out and saw the text message from Hope. It was telling him to come because she'd found Nathan Mackie on the path towards the River Ness

Islands. Of course, he knew the area well, but he wondered why she wanted him. After all, if she'd only found him, then she was going to talk to Nathan Mackie. Something must be wrong.

He started the engine, flicked on the lights, and pulled out into the quiet street. Kyle Mackie would have to wait, but at least he would have somebody with him while Ross wasn't there.

The city was relatively busy and it took a short while for Ross to get there. As Ross moved through the heavy traffic, another text message came in from Hope saying that there were more people here than she thought. Another one said she required backup and was calling it in. Ross could feel his heart begin to pound. *This wasn't normal. If Hope was calling in like this, something was really up.*

He pressed his foot down, driving faster, weaving in and out of the traffic, but he also pressed the phone, calling the station. The sergeant picking up the call advised Ross that Sergeant McGrath hadn't phoned in and hadn't called for backup. Ross insisted he needed some now to rendezvous at the Ness Islands. He didn't know where exactly, but that was where the sergeant had been previously.

Pulling up at one of the streets alongside the river, Ross ran across the small bridge that connected to the little island in the middle of the river. He slowed down his pace, looking around to see the occasional evening walker out and about. There was a man with a dog, a couple so engrossed in themselves they were lucky they didn't walk into a lamppost. There was a family bustling into a car. His glance towards the Ness Islands, however, showed them to be quiet and with no lights showing out there. He didn't know, however, what he would find when

79

he went onto the stretch of heavy vegetation in the midst of the quite-fast-flowing river.

Ross called Hope, but the phone just rang out. He looked around for the arriving backup and did not see any, so he made his way across the bridge onto the first little island. Over by the street, there were enough lights that you could see quite clearly, but out on the islands, you could hear the rush of the water but see so very little. The vegetation closed in before you, trees half craning across paths cutting out the light that shone from across in the street. You got the occasional shadow, the occasional glance of something moving, but you were never sure what it was, a leaf, a branch, a person.

Ross ploughed on down the main path wondering if he should call out. After all, he was the police. Maybe he could cause a reaction, but there was no backup here yet. If there was a large number of them, they could turn on him. It might be best to stay quiet and assess the situation first of all.

Ross met another little bridge taking him across to the second island, and it was then at the far end he thought he saw movement. He crouched down and decided to head off the path into the vegetation. Just as he got into the greenery, somebody ran past him.

'Hurry up, will you; hurry up?'

'She's a struggler. That's the problem,' said a voice.

'I don't care. We need to tidy up and get out. Get rid of her.'

Ross decided to step out of the vegetation. He was assuming that the 'her' was Hope, and he didn't like the way 'get rid of her' was phrased. It sounded terminal. It sounded like someone was going to finish his boss.

Once back out in the path, he could see several men at the far end of it. Two were standing facing each other, holding a long object between them. He could see the legs wrapped together on one end and shoulders at the other. The two men began to swing the figure backwards and forwards before tossing it out into the river.

'Oi, police!' shouted Ross. 'You're surrounded.'

The two men looked up at him, looked over to a third, and they began to run. Ross raced over to where they'd thrown somebody in the water but didn't see the man who was hiding behind one of the bushes. He stepped out, caught Ross across the shins, causing him to fall to the ground. The man then kicked him hard, twice in the stomach, before running off.

Ross doubled up in pain, clutching his stomach tight. The wind was driven out of him, and he started to gasp for breath, but he had to get up. Somebody had gone into that river; somebody had gone in. He wondered if it was the boss.

He knew Hope was a good swimmer. Well, they tied her up. If she was unconscious, she'd never make it out. He rolled up onto his knees, breathing heavily, sucking in large gasps of air, trying to get himself back to some sort of normal condition.

Where was that backup? he thought. Standing up, he took off his jacket, dropped it on the ground, and kicked off his shoes. He looked out into the dark patches of water, occasionally gleaming as a streetlight caught it. He looked around, saw the life ring sitting at the edge of the path, and grabbed it.

Ross stuck it over his head, ran forward, and jumped out into the river. The first thing that struck him was the cold as it raced up his legs and he could feel it in his stomach. He was thrown about, for while the river was not that choppy, it was strong. He bounced about over the reasonably small waves, getting splashed occasionally in the face, but his eyes were scanning downstream, looking to see the person who

81

had just been thrown in. Then he saw her, less than fifteen metres away, but rolling on down the river just as he was.

With both of his arms holding onto the outside of the life ring, Ross kicked hard with his feet, trying to change his direction. After a bit, he found that if he simply manoeuvred his legs and held them like some kind of rudder, he would drift back across towards the person he'd seen. As he got closer, kicking like crazy as he needed to try and speed up his progress, he could see the red hair, the ponytail, lying on top of the water. It took him a while longer, but he was able to reach over and grabbed the leather jacket.

He knew then it was Hope, and he pulled the woman close, lifting her head up onto the top of the life ring. He now tried to adjust his legs and also Hope's body to form some rudder to take them back to the shore. It wasn't easy, and a couple of times he simply spun around. As the river widened slightly, he found himself able to steer better as the current slowed, and they drifted over gently towards the water's edge.

Here he was stuck, for he'd come up against a wall and not a bank. One of his hands reached out, grabbing onto a piece of tree that was growing out from the wall above. Pulling it, he looked up and started shouting out for anyone. He had one hand on Hope, one hand on the tree, and was in dire need of assistance. A face of an elderly man peered over, and for a moment, almost fell backward, stunned.

'What are you doing, son?' he asked.

'Police officer, I need help. I need help, get me people here now!'

Ross continued to hold tight, but he could feel the cold travelling his body, and he wasn't sure how long he could keep his muscles in such a firm hold. Soon with his grip slipping, he also realised that he didn't know how Hope was. Was she breathing? She certainly was unconscious because she made absolutely no effort to speak, to move, nothing.

The elderly man's face had disappeared, and Ross wondered what was going on. He heard a couple of cars pass and wondered why the old man hadn't stopped them. Then he heard the siren and saw the blue lights in the distance, but of course, they stopped further up. He was well down past the islands now, so far away from them. Maybe the old man could bring them down to him. *You have to hurry, have to hurry.*

With one hand, Ross let go of Hope and instead grabbed her arm. He took it and wound it through the life ring just in case they floated off and he couldn't hold her. She should stay afloat then. She'd stay upright with her head out of the water; that's what he surmised.

He believed his right foot had gone numb, tried to find it, tried to swing it, but there was no feeling. It was just as he thought he was probably going to end up letting go, that a silhouetted face arrived, peering over the top again, but this time in a police uniform.

'Get me out, get us out,' said Ross. 'Get an ambulance, too.'

Ross was not that far down from the roadside, but it required three constables to reach over, lying flat, with people holding them, to then reach for Ross and Hope. They got hold of the pair and slowly pulled them up and onto the roadside, up above the river. Ross had a thermal blanket placed around him, but it didn't stop the cold.

He saw an ambulance crew attending to Hope. When they didn't start pounding her chest, looking for it to restart, Ross gave a smile. *She can't have been that bad, or, well, unless she's actually . . .* The thought crossed his mind, but then he saw her head move. It was a roll of the eyes, and she muttered a few words to the ambulance worker with her.

Ross was helped up and placed into the back of an ambulance, which at least was warmer. Suddenly, it dawned on him, like his mind had unfrozen, and he shouted for one of the constables to come to him.

'There were men on the island; you need to do a sweep.'

'Men, what did they look like?' asked the constable. 'Who am I looking for?'

'I don't know,' said Ross, 'but at least two of them threw the sergeant into the water. They might still be about; you need to do a sweep. You need to do a sweep.'

He was aware he was almost rambling, but he was the figure in charge of the investigation with Hope out of action, and he was gradually losing it.

'You need to call the DCI, DCI Lawson. We need him now.' Ross suddenly lay back on the temporary bed inside the ambulance, his eyes closed, and he wondered if they'd given him anything, but soon he started to drift asleep.

Chapter 11

Alan Ross could hear the rushing of the water as he stood at the riverside staring back out at the islands he'd been on so recently, and where all the action had taken place. The ambulance had checked him over and he managed to dry down and receive a change of clothing he held within the station, run down to him by one of the constables. He hadn't wanted to leave the scene unsupervised with Hope incapacitated. He was the senior officer until the DCI arrived.

How much the DCI would take charge, Ross didn't know, and he wondered if the man actually knew what he would do. Hope was in the back of an ambulance, the last he'd seen of her. He thought she'd regained consciousness, but he only saw her from a distance. He thought her eyes were open; someone was talking to her. He doubted she would be let go to see him. If she'd gone unconscious, they'd want to watch her through the night. Surely, that was the least protocol to follow, wasn't it? He wasn't too sure when it came to medical matters but she could do with her rest.

Part of him was angry. Angry they had been left on their own. There was no backup. There was just the two of them, suddenly having to cover all bases, suddenly having to protect people, and not having the full weight of the department behind them.

Ross had spoken to the uniformed sergeant who arrived on scene, talked to him about sealing off the islands, making sure that everything was protected as it was a crime scene, but the man knew what he was doing. The arrival of Jona Nakamura gave Ross a warm glow. She was part of the team even though she didn't work directly for them, and the first thing the woman had done was race over to Ross to ask how Hope was.

The two women were good friends and Jona's face of concern was alleviated somewhat when Ross told her that Hope was in good hands. He wasn't expecting the handshake from Jona. She said the uniformed officers had explained how Ross had saved Hope, pulled her from the water, and held on until they could get her back out. Without him, she may have been dead. Ross hadn't thought about that. He'd just done what was needed. Dived in after someone in trouble and then tried to warm himself up afterwards.

Jona disappeared off to get at her work and Ross felt the anger growing when he saw the car of the DCI arrive. Warren got out of his car, marched over to Ross with almost a grin on his face.

'I see you're on top of things, Ross. Just fill me in on exactly what happened.'

Ross grimaced but mentally prepared himself to run things through in this normal fashion.

'Well, we had two people we needed to protect, sir. I went after one, Kyle Mackie, who's currently in his house with a woman and probably sleeping the night away in a far better fashion than me. The other, Nathan Mackie, we haven't found.

Detective Sergeant McGrath saw Nathan Mackie, or at least thought she did and then a lot more men closed in around her. She sent the message calling for help, told me she was going to call for backup. I followed through with a call to make sure that backup was on its way, but they hadn't received any message.

'When I got here, they were numerous men on the island. I hid for a moment, then I saw the sergeant being thrown into the water and some brief scuffles and then I joined the fray after seeing her being thrown into the river. I jumped in after Hope and I managed to get her to shore where a kindly old man helped us get out when the backup arrived. It was close, sir.'

'Are you on top of what's going on now?'

'The sergeant who has come down has done an excellent job,' said Ross. 'Her team are spreading out. They're taking statements from people. The scene is closed off. Jona Nakamura is here dealing with the forensics. I've got a new change of clothes and actually, I'm feeling okay. Thanks for asking.'

'Where's Hope?'

'Sergeant McGrath is in the back of the ambulance over there and I'm going over to speak to her. I don't know if she's all right or not, but as they haven't raced off to the hospital, I'm presuming she will be at some point.'

'But, of course, Ross, absolutely. I'm sure she'll be fine,' said the DCI. 'I'll expect a full report in the morning.'

'I think our priority is to try and find Nathan Mackie, sir. I've sent uniform back towards his house, but they haven't said anything about him coming back. Kyle Mackie's house is also being watched by uniform. Once again, I'd like to commend the efforts of the sergeant on scene.'

'Of course, Ross. Absolutely. Well, talk to Hope. Get a full report to me in the morning about this. Come and see me, then I can work out what we should do.'

'I take it I'm okay to pull in some more people. We're going to need a manhunt for Nathan Mackie, get to him before anybody else does.'

'You're pulling a lot of resources as it is, Ross. I think you have plenty here. Give me a call if anything else comes up.' The man turned almost dismissively.

'Excuse me, sir,' said Ross. 'If I may, I think you're taking this rather lightly.'

'You have a man that's missing, one the sergeant's been after, and gone into the water. We've recovered the sergeant. She is okay. The man is missing. Everyone else has disappeared. Best to scour the scene, try to pick up what clues we've got. It's now heading towards midnight. I doubt we're going to get much more done tonight. In fact, probably best if you get off home soon too.'

'But not before I fill in the paperwork, sir,' said Ross. 'I'll probably have to go back to the station, then I'll see my bed before the back of three or four.'

'Dedication to the job, Alan Ross. No wonder Macleod liked you. I'm getting to like you myself.' Lawson turned away, marching towards his car and Ross found himself spitting on the ground where the man had stood, and anger was welling up on him. His real boss, as Ross saw it, was currently out of the job, currently having to do everything that went against his own standards, outside of the force and his direct boss was sitting in the back of an ambulance due to a lack of backup. Ross was not happy. He turned, made his way towards the ambulance, knocked on the door, which opened to a green-uniformed woman.

'It's Detective Constable Ross. Detective Sergeant McGrath is my boss. I was just coming to ask if she's okay. If there's any chance I can speak to her?'

'Come on in,' said the woman. 'Hope is going to be fine but she's not going to be staying here. As a precaution, we're going to need to take her to the hospital for overnight. Just precaution, nothing else, just because she went unconscious. She said you saved her.'

'Yes,' said Ross. 'Your colleague checked me over. I'm fine. I was in the water, but once I warmed up, I was okay. I didn't swallow anything, so I'm okay.'

'I was going to say well done,' said the woman. 'She probably owes you her life.'

'Well,' said Ross, 'She's probably saved mine at some point. Is it okay if I talk to her alone? I don't mean to push you out, but there's some details that you really shouldn't be privy to.'

'I understand.' The woman turned and shouted to her partner. 'John, come on. Give you five minutes. Not much longer though. I want to get Hope to the hospital and get her down for the night.'

Ross thanked the woman, watched while her partner left the ambulance and closed the door behind him. He turned to see Hope, lying on the bed, wrapped up under blankets. Her red hair was splayed around the pillow. The ponytail had been undone.

'Are you okay?' asked Ross.

'Has anyone told John?' she said.

'Not yet. You were okay. I didn't think it was . . .'

'Good, because he'll worry. You worry at these things.'

89

'You'll have to tell him you're going into the hospital though.'

'Then he'll come up,' said Hope, 'when really I just need to sleep.'

'I'll take it,' said Ross. 'I'll deal with him. Tell him to come in, maybe pick you up about nine or ten tomorrow.'

'Are you okay?' asked Hope. 'I feel like I'm just handing you everything here, while I go off for a sleep.'

'I'm fine,' said Ross. 'Look at me. New outfit, new shoes, and the DCI has gone home. What could be better in life?'

'Thanks,' said Hope. 'We really need to rethink this.'

'What do you mean?' asked Ross, half sitting on the mobile bed.

'We're charging at this. We're trying to do this, and we're under-resourced even before we were short of Clarissa. Climbing onto that roof, falling down, hurting her ankle. Now she is off tearing around with the boss. We're exposed at the moment. We're doing this without the cover we normally have. And something else.'

'What?' asked Ross.

'The DCI, how long did he stay?'

'Five minutes if we're lucky. Sergeant Maughan is very good; she's covering off very well. I haven't got any worries about the scene or what we're doing.'

'No, but I'm down. I'm being taken away and I'll expect Lawson's leaving a DC to cover this. There's no inspector. There's not even a sergeant. Yes, uniform are here. They're doing a job but there should be a DCI or DI or DS over the top of this. Somebody tried to kill me. I reported that I was protecting someone. The man really is very, very sloppy or . . .'

'You think he's got some reason? You think he's protecting

somebody?'

'I have no idea,' said Hope. 'Seoras never would've left. Not unless he had somewhere to go involved with the case and he would've left me covering. We have plenty of other detective sergeants in other groups that could have been pooled in.'

'Well, don't worry about it at the moment,' said Ross. 'I'll be all right tonight. What happened with you though?'

'Well, I thought I saw a man with a Labrador. I thought I saw Nathan Mackie. I watched from a distance and then he's onto the islands. When I went onto the islands, there are these other people there. I emerged onto the path from the undergrowth and got cut off and attacked. They hit my head and I blacked out. Then I'm told that you got me out of the water. You were hanging onto me.'

'Yes, I was. I saw them throw you in. Had a bit of a scuffle getting in after you. I managed to get a life ring and jumped in. I hung on to you, got your hands attached to it, hung on at the side and some old bloke went and got our backup down to us.'

'You called backup?'

'I checked if you got through and what was coming because suddenly, you weren't speaking to me. We got you though. We got you.'

'Give me a minute,' said Hope. He shifted himself off the bed, walked up and leaned over her. Hope removed her bare arms from underneath the covers, wrapped them around his neck, pulling him close and kissed him on the cheek. She then hugged him tight and he could hear the tears coming.

'You saved me. Thank you. I was gone. Thank you.'

Ross was in a rather uncomfortable position and didn't know what to say, merely remaining bent over until Hope released him. As she did so, he saw the tears in the eyes and the smile on her face.

'You'd do the same for me,' said Ross. He straightened up and readjusted his tie. 'You need to get off to the hospital. Don't worry about anything until the morning. I'll talk to John and get him there. Only when he's picked you up and they've said you're okay, you start to think about this again. I'll phone in for some of the extras we pull in at times. I'll sort it. It's not that big a deal. It's just a crime scene. It's not like there's a body to pick up.'

Hope looked up solemnly at Ross. 'I think there will be. I think they've already done it. Just that things they said seem very final. I don't think I was someone interrupting them. I think I might have been there to discover a body.'

'Well, they haven't found anything on the islands. I checked. They're still being searched and I'll look after the search as well; don't you worry about that. You get off. I'll try and call Clarissa when I get a chance. Update the boss.'

Hope nodded, put her arms back in underneath the covers and started to slip off to sleep.

Ross exited the back of the ambulance, thanked the paramedics again, telling them they were free to leave whenever they wanted, and he marched over towards Sergeant Maughan dealing with the situation. As he got close, he saw her talk quickly into her radio comms. As she glanced up, she saw him and waved him over quickly.

'Get in the car, Ross. They've found something.'

Ross jumped into the back of a marked police car and was driven along at speed down to the far end of the river where there was a blue flashing light and an ambulance arriving as well. Ross jumped out, followed Maughan to the riverbank but kept a distance while the paramedics attended to what looked like a body. After a few minutes, one of the paramedics stood up and shook his head.

'He's gone. Long dead. Looking at him, I don't think he drowned. I think he was killed before, but I'll leave that up to your forensics to establish. But he's not alive.'

Ross took out his phone, found a photograph he had of Nathan Mackie as someone shone a torch in the man's face. Ross realised it was the same person.

'Okay, Sergeant Maughan, this is the person that Sergeant McGrath was looking for. I suggest you corner the area off. I'll contact Jona. Better seal off what's around. I suggest you fan out, see if anyone's about, but I'd tell them to be careful. These people are killers. They appear to even be killing their own.'

Maughan looked over at him grimly, nodded, turned away, and started to bark orders through a radio. Ross stepped back from the body up onto the roadside, looking down towards the river. From the bushes, he heard something, and he turned towards the sound, hearing a whimper but it wasn't human. He saw a dog on the riverbank, a Labrador. The animal was wounded but Ross couldn't tell how badly. He turned and shouted up to Maughan, 'Get a vet down here ASAP, please. I think I found his dog.'

Ross sat down beside the dog, taking off his jacket and putting it over the animal. It didn't seem to be moving. He rubbed his hand behind its neck and across up behind its ears. He looked back over at its owner. Inside the anger was mounting. *That could have been Hope*, he thought. *That could have been Hope.*

Chapter 12

The green sports car pulled off the motorway heading into the north of Glasgow. As happened in Glasgow, they passed from a poor area to rather posh area in a matter of a few streets. Macleod remembered how areas were distinct, yet so close to each other. Taking a wrong turn or wandering into a bad area was the easiest thing to do. It was one of the things he liked about Glasgow; in some ways, it was an equaliser. You all get on the same bus after all, passing through each area.

He watched Clarissa take two lefts and then a right and consult her phone again, which was navigating to the house they wanted. She stopped down the street, some distance away from a large house at the end with a pair of iron gates. Macleod could see several men around the gates and knew they must have arrived at the correct place.

'Let me take this,' said Macleod. 'This was my world. It's never been yours. They don't operate the same as the art world, I would believe. They can be a lot colder, a lot more barbaric.'

'Did you get a lot of these when you were back down here?'

'Oh yes,' said Macleod. 'Got a lot of gangland killings. These guys here don't like me, really don't like me, and that's fair enough because I don't like them either, but I need them. Otherwise, I wouldn't come within a hundred miles of this place. Not unless I was on a case.'

Clarissa looked at him, slightly worried and watched him pull his hoodie up, dragging it around his face. She thought that was the cue to drive forward and plonk the car up in front of the main driveway with the iron gates beyond. A rather sour-faced individual with a sharp jaw and chin almost growled at her. She leaned over the side of the door. 'Wondering if you guys could help me,' said Clarissa politely.

'No problem, hen, but by the way, sod off.'

'I think you'll want to talk,' said Clarissa.

'Which part of sod off didn't you hear, hen? Not a place for a woman like you. Go on, get.'

Clarissa glared at the man, and then sat back in the car. Macleod pulled down his hoodie, simply turned and stared at the man. He saw him take a step back almost in shock. Then he waved over to another man by the gate. He came over to the car.

'What the hell are you doing here? Didn't think you'd have the cheek to show your face around here. It's not a safe place for a piece of turd like yourself.'

Macleod didn't flinch, instead he flicked his eyes towards the man and then simply said, 'I'm here to see the boss. Get me the boss.'

'Hey,' said the other guy, 'you don't go around making demands like that.'

'Use your brains. I'm here to see the boss. You think I'd be here if it wasn't important?'

'Yes, you might be here to bust him now, mightn't you? You can get lost.'

'To bust him?' said Macleod. 'It's no wonder he gives you gate duty. If I was here to bust him, there'd be cars, lots of squad cars down here. Plenty of them, now get on that intercom and tell your boss, Macleod's here and he wants to speak.'

'What if the boss says no?' asked the other man.

'Your boss won't say no,' said Macleod. 'That's why he's the brains of the outfit. Now hurry up and get, before I let this woman beside me loose.'

The two men looked at each other for a moment, then looked at Clarissa, who simply gave them an evil smile. There was no way Macleod was ever going to put her into that danger. There was no way he'd ever put her up against them. But it didn't do any harm in their thinking that if things came to it, they'd have to give her a wide steer.

Macleod sat in silence as he watched the man approach the gate intercom. He called for a moment and then stood waiting, tapping his feet. Of course, the boss wasn't on the end of that line. They'd have to go and get him, but he'd come running up in the end. Macleod was sure of that.

There was a momentary hesitation from the man at the intercom when the voice spoke to him and then he marched over to the little green sports car and waved at those on the gate to start to open them.

'He says he wants to make sure it's you. Drive the sports car up. Stick your face in the camera.'

'Tell him it was the Wrath of God he offended, not me. Tell him he brought it all down on himself.'

The man looked a little bit worried for a moment and said to Macleod, 'No, you need to go to the intercom. The boss has asked you to go and put your face in the camera.'

Macleod opened the car door, stepped out. 'With me,

sunshine,' he said, and walked towards the video camera. As he approached it, the other man stood close beside them and Macleod grabbed him by the ear, pulling him up to the camera and jabbing his thumb in up underneath his ribs. 'Tell him what I said.'

The man struggled to breathe, but then he said, 'God, wrath, offended. Not fault.' Macleod shoved him away, the man breathing heavily, trying to recover. Macleod looked over at the video camera.

'I'm coming in. I need to talk with you.'

He didn't wait for a reply. Marching over to the sports car, he told Clarissa to drive. She did so and began the long winding driveway up to the high house on the hill. He saw her looking over, watching his hands shaking like crazy.

'Good show,' said Clarissa. 'It was a good show. What about inside?'

'Leave the talking to me; we don't want to get into any nonsense here. This guy's a killer. It'll be a heck of a risk we're undertaking at the moment. They won't lay a finger on you or me because he knows what I can do. He also knows you're well-liked in the force, so they'll come after him.'

Clarissa gave a laugh. 'Now you're just making things up.'

'Seriously though,' said Macleod, 'best behaviour. Don't react quickly. Don't take offense. I'll tell you if all hell's broke loose, and we may need to do something.'

Closing his eyes, he gave a brief prayer and opened them as Clarissa pulled the car up to large steps before the house. There were large marble pillars and the door opened. Macleod saw a man coming through he recognised. Gleary's henchman. They had crossed paths before.

'Ricardo,' said Macleod. 'Well, he sent you to guide me in.

That's very kind of him. How long did you spend in there?'

'Ten years for you, you bastard,' said the man. 'Ten damn years, and he makes me walk you in. I should knife you where you stand.'

'You're not that bright though, are you? You don't know when and where, how to do it. You shouldn't let people squeal on you.'

'I shouldn't have worked with people you run rings around, more like. Get out of the car.'

'Lady's present,' said Macleod.

The henchman looked over. 'What the hell is that?'

'I warn you, she bites,' said Macleod.

They got out of the car and closed the door. 'With me, Urquhart,' he said, using her second name because Clarissa sounded all too friendly. The henchman didn't look back, but led them through a large set of double doors to a rather elaborate hallway, then into a study with wood panelling and pictures of family. There was a settee on the far side and henchman simply pointed at it.

'I won't ask you if you want a drink. I take it you still don't touch the stuff.'

'Devil's Brew,' said Macleod. 'Devil's Brew. And she's driving.'

The pair were then left inside. Clarissa wanted to speak, but Macleod put his hand up. He whispered softly, 'They're probably watching us wondering why we're here. It's what they do. But look, this one's got a window to the outside. There's a video camera up the corner. That's all good.'

'Why?' asked Clarissa.

'If we've got video and a window to the outside, it's not a kill room.'

'A what?'

'A kill room. If you're going to kill somebody, you don't want to put it on video. You don't want to have somebody pop up at the window and see you do it either. You do it in a room that's in the middle of the house, one which people can then come in and clean. This is not a kill room. It's going well.'

'Did you think we might have ended up in one?'

'Can never be sure,' said Macleod, 'but I'd be telling you to do something by now if we had.'

The door opened and an old man strolled into the room. He had grey hair, slicked onto his head by some gel. His eyes had large bags underneath and he looked weary. He had a belly on him hanging down over his belt and he seemed to half shuffle instead of walk.

'How the hell are you still going?' asked the man. 'What's this? You dare to walk into my house after what you did to me.'

'You did it to yourself, or rather your family did. If you had just buried them. You had to just simply dispatch them, but no, you had to torture, and you had to torture in a fancy way. Wasn't difficult to trace.'

'What the hell do you want, Macleod? Anyway, I see they've kicked you out. I see you got that one wrong. You made a bollocks of that, didn't you?'

'You watch the telly, you read the papers, do you?' said Macleod. 'Well, problem is, I didn't make a mess of it. They've made a mess of it.'

The man stared at him, and he shook his head. 'What the hell is that to do with me?'

'We took on a case in which three kids died. Symbols carved on them. Satanic symbols, symbols from other cultures, meaning death. One of the mothers was killed as well, but by accident. We were hunting down child killers. We took a long-lost soul into custody and he hung himself and they said, 'There's our man.' It's not. The knives are still out on the go. Knives. Knives I think you transported. Knives that are used to kill children.

'You always told me children were never involved. You always told me you wouldn't do that. When you took Nickles down, you waited until his son was out of the building. You're a right bastard,' said Macleod, 'you're an evil man in a lot of ways, but you don't let that happen to children.'

Macleod stood up and pointed to the wall. There was a picture there of extended family and the old man was in the middle.

'Look at all the kids around there. Your grandkids, your great-grandkids, a lot of them.'

Macleod saw the anger in the man's face. 'It's not me,' he said, 'I don't go in for that sort of thing. I didn't know they're being used for kids. Are you sure it's the knives we moved?'

Macleod pointed to Clarissa. 'She worked in that line, good on the artistic side of things. She found them. We traced them and they come from you.'

'Well, it wasn't me that moved them,' he said. 'It's my niece. You make me wonder who she was dealing with. She's modern. You know, it's not like we were, Macleod. Rob a bank, that's the money in your hand. Now you've got to move the drugs. Now you've got to extort here or there, wherever. Lot of people, child traffic, and that nonsense. It's not proper crime. There's nothing honourable in it.'

'I never saw the honour in any of it,' said Macleod.

The man almost raged at him, but then he turned and

marched over to whiskey counter with two crystal glasses. He poured the drink into both of them. He knocked the one back, gave a gasp, the burning sensation in his throat, and then he held the other one in front of Macleod.

'This is for the one you can't have.' He downed it as well.

'Where is she?' Macleod asked. 'Where's this niece?'

The man looked over at Macleod. 'They kicked you out. They kicked you out. Who the hell didn't listen to you and kicked you out? They did that once down here. Do you remember? You almost had me. You almost had me, and they wouldn't listen to you. I'll bet you hated them that day.'

Macleod's face didn't flinch. 'Where is she? I'll tell them. I'll tell them all. I'll tell them all that Gleary facilitated the deaths of children, tortured children, Satanic marks cut onto the backs of children. Who knows what else they'll do to them.'

Gleary looked at him, pushed a hand through his greying hair, thin as it was across the top of his head. 'I'll take you to her,' said Gleary. 'We'll go, and we'll have a chat. We'll find out who your knives belong to, and you can sort them out, but you leave her alone.'

'As long as she's not the one wielding the knife,' said Macleod, 'that'll work for me.'

'She's not wielding the knife. She wouldn't know how to. That's the trouble these days. They're all into this nonsense and they don't know how to use the old, good, simple tools of the trade. You don't know what it's like trying to get good staff today, Macleod. You have no idea. Now come on. And you leave her here.'

'Why?' asked Macleod.

'Security. I don't want you pulling any fast ones on me.'

'I don't have a police force behind me,' said Macleod. 'I'm

here talking to the man, out of all people, who probably hates me the most, who'd probably like to take a spade, dig a hole, and put me in it. I'm here for one reason. To stop more of these kids dying and I know you'll go for that.'

The man turned and looked at Clarissa. 'Whatever happened to the other one? Every time I see you in the press, six foot, with a body that rocks, and red hair, and you bring me this. I mean, she's nearly older than you, Macleod.'

'You may be right,' said Macleod. 'But the other one, she doesn't bite the way this one does.' He gave a half turn and saw the faint smile on Clarissa's face.

Chapter 13

Macleod was sitting in the rear of a BMW with tinted windows. Beside him sat Gleary, looking out the window and saying very little. In the front seat was his henchman and a driver Macleod hadn't seen before. Gleary had not been threatening towards him, merely told him to get into the car, and Macleod had kept quiet for he'd no desire to talk to the man. He was a relic of another time, a time where Macleod was not himself, suffering after his wife had killed herself up in Lewis. He had buried himself in his work and then a staunch island conservatism had torn at him and left him highly devoid of affection, humour, and a decency towards everyone around him.

He'd been a swine of a detective. Brutal in the sense that he tore through the obstacles in the way. He learned a lot about how to see into the souls of killers, how to understand what was going on in their minds, how to merely pick up on the little minutiae that told everything. He'd also lost himself in the process and he was thankful the day he met Hope McGrath and that all changed—though he still looked back at the way he'd first reacted to her with a strong sense of shame.

'You said she bites,' said Gleary. 'I heard she was the art

department.'

'You didn't hear anything. You've kept tabs on me the whole time, haven't you? Even when I've been up in Inverness, you know everything. You know my team.'

'Two women and a gay man,' said Gleary. 'I never put you down for that. The Macleod that left here wouldn't have done that. They would've been devil's things.'

'I'd say I know the devil's things a lot more clearly these days,' said Macleod, 'and what I've seen with the knives and these children, they are the devil's things.'

'You were one of the few I couldn't bribe, do you know that? You know that half your department was in my pocket?'

'Of course, I did,' said Macleod. 'That's why half of them had to leave.'

'Yes, you screwed me up for a while. You really did. That's the thing. You would always be on a job because the crime always comes back. People can't get enough of it. There's always a reason for it, always time to extort or to bribe. Crime isn't the heartbeat of the human condition. It's the blood flow,' said Gleary.

'The poison that seeps in, more like. You weren't that stupid. You were a clever man. You could have led people. You could have done something good. Look at me. What did I have? I could just tell you. I could just see what's been done. That's why I was the detective.'

'I'm still quite disappointed,' said Gleary. 'Fancy meeting that redhead you had and you picked another one. What is it? Just not like normal blokes since you left.'

'I don't pick my team on what they look like,' said Macleod. 'I pick my team on what they can do. Your supposed gay man is what holds our team together. As for the women on my team, the redhead that I haven't brought will be the one to take over and she will be better than me, Gleary. You have anybody you can say that about? The one I left at your house, if I don't come back, she'll torch the place.'

'You're winding me up,' said Gleary. 'You don't have to talk tough. We know who you are.'

'You know I'm not lying. She'd torch the place if you do anything to me. She'd wreck a vengeance the other two wouldn't have a clue about. Detective Clarissa Urquhart is old school and she is a tough nugget.'

'It was a glad day the day you moved up there,' said Gleary. 'A very glad day. We haven't found a wily bastard like you. At least not yet.'

The pair continued in silence as the car swept into a rather depressing set of tower blocks. Macleod glanced out of the window, saw them rising high up into the sky. Looking around, he saw a couple of shopping trolleys, people stumbling about, some not able to focus, others with bottles of spirits in their hand, others with tinnies. Cheap lager from down the off-license.

'She lives in the classy part of town then.'

'Business,' said Gleary. 'She lives amongst her customers. I wish it were different. She's not normally a courier. Certainly wouldn't be for that sort of thing.'

'Well, why is she doing it then?' said Macleod.

'When I heard, I thought it was just one of these daft things she's heavily into, I don't know, what do you call it? Is it metal music? I have no idea what it is today. Rock music, pop music. Sounds like noise to me. But these people here, they suck it up along with the drugs and the booze. She's got a good market here. She's at the top of one of the trees. Let's go pay a visit.'

Gleary got out of the car and didn't wait for Macleod, instead marching straight over to the doors of one of the tower blocks. Macleod saw a couple of men moving to block him, young, no more than twenty, and Gleary's henchman stepped in front. He cracked one with a punch to the face, dropping him instantly. The other, he put a flick-knife out to, holding it up to the man's throat and telling him to get the hell out of the way. Gleary turned around.

'Are you coming?'

Macleod followed and watched as they made it up to the next floor where some guns were pulled out. Gleary's henchman stepped forward.

'I suggest you call your boss, Miss Amanda, on the top floor. This is her uncle. If those guns are not away from him in the next five seconds, he'll personally make sure that each one of you dies.'

Macleod could see the hesitation, the worry, and guns were lowered, if not quite put back in holsters. It took several minutes for voice communications to go from upstairs to downstairs and then suddenly the steps up were clear.

'Thought at our age we could take the lift.'

'What?' said Gleary. 'And get stuck in it? Have it suddenly descend quickly to the floor?'

'Thought you said it was your niece.'

'Yes. She's one of mine. Taught her well; she could take over. You love them for it but you've got to be careful.'

Macleod didn't know what to think but trudged up the many steps to the floor at the very top of the high-rise flat. As he climbed, he could see drug dealers at the doors, making transactions. There were also groups of women that clearly were there to sell themselves. This was not where Macleod wanted to be. If he had been on formal duty, he would have torn into the place. He must mention it someplace, drop a line to Glasgow about it.

When they reached the top floor, the henchman stopped. Gleary continued on his own, opening a large wooden door and shouting inside.

'Mandy, are you in? Where are you, hen?'

Macleod walked into an incredibly dark flat, looking at the walls, with images, many of them bloody, like a horror movie scene. He also noticed the upside-down crosses on the wall.

His blood ran cold looking at them, and he thought back to the kids who would have been carved on. There was a lot of occult books on the shelves, but Macleod kept to himself as Gleary continued to walk inside.

'Amanda, are you in?'

Macleod nearly collapsed when he saw the woman who walked around towards him. She had on a pair of long boots, and then what Macleod would have thought was a nightgown. It was black with thin lace material, and you could see that underneath she wore only bottoms. It was anything but attractive. Around her neck he could see the upside-down cross hanging from it, mocking him. Macleod put the girl at no more than about twenty-five. He watched Gleary staring at her as she stumbled over towards him.

'Uncle, what the hell are you doing here? You don't need to be here.'

'I can come when I want, can't I? Mandy, what's going on?'

'I don't know what you mean,' she said. Macleod could see the whiskey tumbler in her hand. He also saw a line of veins that had been punctured recently, in her upper arm.

'I asked you a question,' said Gleary. 'Mandy, what's going

on? What's going on with these knives?'

'None of your bloody business,' she said. 'That was a transaction between me and my client. They're all gone. All gone off and been delivered. You don't need to stick your nose into my business.'

'Your business?' said the man. 'You're lucky you have a business. Tell me now, hen, who ordered the movement of the knives?'

'Not telling you that,' he said.

'You're trying my patience,' said Gleary. 'You really are.'

He reached over, grabbed the gown she was wearing, pulling her close to him. Macleod stood at a distance, watching Gleary pull her up to his face.

'Where did you take them?'

'Why? What do you care about it for? Who the hell is this?'

'This is a man who's been chasing down the murderer of young children. He says our knives have been used carving details into a lot of kids. It's not what we get involved in, you know that. I always told you that business is business, but you don't bring the little ones into it. What have you done?'

'Don't need to tell you anything,' said Amanda. Gleary grabbed her, hauling her over to the window that he threw open, and then started to haul her out of it.

'Hey,' said Macleod, but Gleary turned around and told him to shut the hell up. Macleod watched as he smacked the woman several times around the face. Then he had his hand on her throat. Macleod wanted to go forward, but there was a cough from outside the door. Gleary's henchman was watching, keeping an eye. There was no way Macleod could intervene without being incapacitated by the man. Macleod watched as Gleary began to tip her feet up, and he wondered if he would drop her straight out of the window.

'Don't take the piss on me,' said Gleary. 'Those knives, where did they go?'

'Don't worry about that,' she shouted. Macleod heard people running towards the room, and then there was a scuffle outside. A youth came racing through beside Macleod, his head slamming into the wall. He collapsed unconscious on the ground.

Meanwhile, Gleary had his niece's legs up in the air, so her gown was falling unceremoniously around her.

'Don't do it,' said Macleod.

'I won't tell you again. Shut the hell up. This is my place. This is my way.'

Macleod was thinking about stepping over, but outside he saw the henchman pull back his jacket, letting Macleod see the gun. There was too much animosity there and Ricardo could gun him down.

The girl was choking now. He saw Gleary smack her several more times, each time with the back of his hand, right across her cheeks. By the time he pulled her back up, there were tears in her eyes, and she flopped onto the bed nearby. Macleod made his way over, and knelt in front of her.

'What do you know?' he asked. 'Tell me what you know.'

'You heard the Inspector,' said Gleary. 'He wants to know what happened to the knives.'

'They didn't show themselves to me,' said Amanda. 'They just organised it. Drop notes. There's nothing I can tell you.'

'You can tell me where you dropped it,' said Macleod. 'Even though you might not have seen them.' Macleod pulled out a notepad. 'You've got to deliver it somewhere. Where did you deliver it?'

For a moment, this seems to flummox the woman. Then she muttered something. Macleod got down close. She gave him an address in Dunkeld. Dunkeld was up near Perth and over an hour away. A good area. Somewhere good to stop if you were trying to move things from south to north. It was right on the main road; while pulling off into it, you were reasonably out of sight of most of the traffic passing along. It sounded like a good place.

'You must step out now, Macleod,' said Gleary. 'I think my niece needs to have a bit of a re-education, a few things explained to her. Ricardo will take you down to the car. He'll drop you somewhere, let your Rottweiler know where you are. By the way, Macleod. I don't want to see your face again. You come into my house again like that and I'll shoot you dead. It's bad enough you put half of my family in prison. Now you show me what this piece of dirt is.'

Macleod knew he was a police officer; he'd have to step in or stop him. The man was clearly going to abuse the girl, beat her or something, but if he tried to stop her in his current position, he'd end up probably dead in a body bag somewhere. Macleod turned on his heel, sick of the dark sight around him, and made his way down the steps all the way to the bottom, his knee joints suffering at every drop. By the time he got down to the bottom, the driver with the car and Ricardo made sure he entered the car quickly. They drove him out to the M8, dropping him at a service station, and Macleod phoned Clarissa.

'Did you get anything?' asked Clarissa on the other end.

'Enough,' said Macleod. 'We've got enough. I hope you won't mind doing a little bit on overtime for this one.'

Chapter 14

The morning following her escapade in the River Ness, Hope McGrath was discharged from Raigmore Hospital, having been watched overnight to make sure there was no longer any ill effects from her unconscious state. She'd been told it was purely precautionary, but she also needed to warm up for the cold had got to her and it was only in the morning that she felt herself again. The shivers had gone, and she was able to smile when her partner John walked into Raigmore hospital with a promised lift home.

He wasn't surprised when she said she'd have to get back to work, although the DCI had sent a message that she could take off as much time as she wanted. On hearing this, Hope had called Ross, unfortunately waking him up after he'd been out most of the night. He told Hope that the DCI hadn't organised anybody else to come in and take over the investigation. He was running it with a very loose rein, and Ross very much felt like he was on his own. Even if Ross hadn't have mentioned this, Hope would have been back because she knew that Macleod and Clarissa were pushing on avenues further south.

Hope breakfasted with John before he ran her over to the River Ness to let her pick up her car. After a swift hug and a kiss, he raced off to the car-hire firm which he had left that morning in the hands of a junior colleague who he wasn't entirely convinced of. Hope went to get into her car but then stopped and walked over to the railings at the edge of the river. There was still police tape up, still some constables on duty protecting the crime scene, and the forensics were still combing through. She could see further down the river another taped-off crime scene.

She wondered when Ross would be out to pick up the pieces. It was what he usually did. While she, Macleod, and Clarissa were running around, Ross was tying off the loose ends. It was what he was good at, but to leave him to front up an investigation, was an action she wasn't entirely convinced by. There was that time in the Monach Isles where he was on his own. Seoras had always said he'd done remarkably well but that was also the time that Ross had been shot, albeit after the back-up had arrived. It was a time she didn't want to remember.

Hope felt herself grabbing the railings tight as her eyes focused on the rushing water. She'd been in there. She'd gone from that island into the water and back out without even knowing it. She'd been compromised so badly that they'd simply tossed her into the river unable to defend herself because of her unconscious state, and then she thought of Clarissa.

I told Macleod that Clarissa had been reckless climbing up on the roof, falling down. Had she been more reckless? Had they been put under the cosh though? The resources hadn't been there. Did that justify putting your own life at risk? *Well*, she thought, *I was trying to save another*. Not that it mattered anymore. Nathan Mackie's body was the one further down, according to Ross. He'd given her a detailed brief by phone that morning, but now it was time for her to take over the investigation, to take charge. To do that, she'd have to handle her DCI.

Hope slipped inside her car, put on the stereo, and heard some modern poppy tune come across the radio, one that she particularly didn't like. She pressed the button on it, allowing her phone to tap in. The Bluetooth connected, and she pressed the song that always woke her up in her younger days, and then hated herself for using that comment because she wasn't that old.

She had dated a bloke into heavy metal, and although she didn't really like the music, she had picked up a few tunes that rang with her. Some of them were quite old, really, well before she was born. Well, she didn't think they'd be the type Seoras would like.

As she put the foot on the accelerator, the chorus rang out, the drums beat out a fast, hard, steady rhythm. She heard the woman begin to sing. She'd always liked Lita Ford's stuff. Also liked the way she looked, and dressed, quite sexy really. Back in the day, she'd have tried to emulate it. Back in the day when she had confidence only in her looks and not in her own abilities or worth. She still liked the look though, even though she wouldn't feel the need to dress like that for a boy. Anyway, she had a car-hire man—she didn't need a metal head.

Many loud and head-banging minutes later, Hope pulled into the car park at the Inverness Police Station, turned off the engine, slipped the key in her pocket, and almost sprang up the stairs inside the building towards DCI Lawson's office. She gave the door a thunderous knock, heard a 'Come in,' and opened it to find the DCI knocking a golf ball across the floor.

A fallen cup at the far end remained undisturbed as the ball sailed at least two inches to the left.

'Did I disturb you?' asked Hope.

'Not at all. Come in. Come in. You're looking well. I thought I told you to take the day off. You've got the hair up in that ponytail again. I take it that means you want to work.'

'I think I need to work, don't I?'

'Why's that?'

'Well,' said Hope, 'Ross has been out all night. He's not got any cover. He's a good guy, but we've just had a murder. We don't have a DI and are down a DS. If you take me out of the equation, are you stepping in, sir?'

Hope used the word 'sir' deliberately, hoping to encourage the man that he actually had a rank that meant he should get off his butt and do something.

'Oh, it's all under control. Ross has done a sterling job. I was just speaking to him about ten minutes ago.'

'You woke him up again,' said Hope.

'Ross doesn't sleep, does he? Tremendous chap. You can see why Macleod liked him. He does pick everything up, doesn't he? I mean, look at the reports he sent through for me. Fabulous. Clearly, we've got a group of people out on the run after this. Nathan Mackie, I thought I'd swing that over to one of the other crime groups. Get somebody else set up on it. We're kind of low numbers as you say.'

'This is our patch,' said Hope. 'Why are we throwing it away to someone else? Why are you forming a murder team when we are here? It's why we formed up in Inverness, so we didn't have to bring people up from Glasgow. I know, I was one of the original ones who came up.'

'Doesn't mean we can't use Glasgow occasionally,' said

Lawson. 'Besides, like you said, we're down several people.'

'I'll cover it,' said Hope. 'Besides, I think it's linked in.'

'You think it's linked in? You told me this cock and bull story the other day and I let you go for the evening on it, but really, you need to stop going down this line.'

'Why?' asked Hope. 'Why do I need to stop going down this line? There's a thread there and that thread needs pulled.'

'What's this thread that needs pulled?'

Hope thought for a minute. She couldn't expose Macleod and Clarissa. She couldn't simply say what they'd been doing. She had already said to the DCI previously that information had come through, but she wasn't going to leak where it was coming from.

'My source, he believes that Nathan Mackie's linked into those earlier murders of the children.'

'What evidence is there for this? Where is this coming from?'

'I can't say at the moment.'

'You can't tell your DCI?'

'I can't expose this person,' said Hope. 'I need to keep it on the quiet if I'm going to get any more information out of them.'

'Well, that's not very satisfactory,' said the DCI, striding across the room, pulling three golf balls back. 'We really can't be going that far on this sort of basis. If you want to work, I'm quite happy for you to take the Nathan Mackie murder. If you think you can handle it with Ross, by all means, but I doubt it's linked into the others.

'We don't need to be doing anything on that front. This has nothing to do with kids. There's no kids killed here. This is a dispute amongst people for whatever reason. Maybe he's got a tenuous link and maybe you'll find that when you see who his murderer is, but we are not going out to the public to say, do you know what? Ian Lamb, we may have got it wrong. He committed suicide in our care. For God's sake, Hope. Do you not care about the department?'

Hope looked up at him fiercely. 'Since when did the department come first?'

'We have to protect ourselves, especially now we've told the public that we've solved that murder and hey, look, I don't see any more children dead. I don't see any more murders. We've probably got the right guy. He took his own life so we didn't have to go through the whole charade of a trial only for him to be found not guilty. Worked out well for us. Very well.'

Hope almost felt sick. Macleod would never tell a soul that the death of anyone worked for him or was a good thing. The one thing her now disgraced boss always believed was that all life was precious. Everybody had a right to change, a right to be someone different than who they were at that point in time. He wasn't stupid enough to think that everybody would, but they deserved the chance.

Hope was struggling with this callousness, this self-preservation. She thought of Clarissa jumping up on those roofs, then nearly falling and breaking her ankle. She wasn't about self-preservation either, nor was Ross, and neither was Hope. *We may have been foolish at times, may have overplayed the hand, not been wise enough to keep ourselves safe, but we wouldn't betray the very thing we were in.*

'What will you do if it turns out Nathan Mackie is the killer?'

'Hasn't turned out, has it? I doubt it will,' said Lawson. 'The more and more you go into these things, Sergeant, the more and more you realise what the answers should be.' Hope watched the man putt, and again the cup was missed by a good two inches on the left-hand side.

'Do you ever think,' said Hope, 'that sometimes you do the same thing over and over again and it gets you the same result? Sometimes you have to look at why things are happening and what's going on.'

'What do you mean?'

'Well,' said Hope, and she stepped forward taking the putter from him. He stood up momentarily as if offended but was a good four inches smaller and found that Hope dwarfed him. She bent her knee slightly for the putter was short, looked along the line to the cup and then up at the DCI.

'You're pulling across the line each time, yet you've hit the putt time and again, from what I've seen, to the left. At no point had you sat and gone, 'What's going on?' because you're doing this.'

She took the first of the balls, struck it, and it went two inches to the left.

'Now if you just adjust what you're doing here and try and follow through a little bit straighter and not cut across the line of the ball, this'll happen.'

Hope contacted the ball and it ran, tripped the edge of the cup, but made its way inside. She held up the putter and handed it back to the DCI.

'You don't get the answer before you do the work to find out why it's that answer,' she said. 'Seoras was doing that. That's why Seoras didn't think Ian Lamb was guilty.'

'He got that wrong,' said the DCI.

'No, Ian Lamb killed himself before Seoras could prove it, and you hung him out to dry. I didn't appreciate that.'

'Watch your tone, Sergeant,' said Lawson. 'If you want to be a DI, you have to speak better than that.'

'I've only ever wanted to be a police officer,' said Hope.

117

'I'll speak what's right. There's more in this Nathan Mackie murder than you believe, and there'll come a time soon when another child will be killed.'

'Can you prove that? What's your evidence for that?'

'My contact's working on it.'

'Who's your contact? Who is this mysterious person you keep telling me about?'

'I won't say because it'll close the investigation. I need to let them operate,' said Hope, 'but they will, and we will resolve this.'

'In the meantime,' said Lawson looking at her, 'you'll get your arse out and get looking into this Nathan Mackie murder. I don't want any crosslinks put forward that aren't justified. Do you understand me, Sergeant?'

'I think we understand each other perfectly,' said Hope. 'Perfectly.' She watched him march across the room, pull back the three golf balls, including the one in the cup, and set them up again.

'If that's all, sir,' said Hope.

'Watch your tone, Sergeant. That's all. I expect to see a report at the end of the day on what you have.'

'Yes, sir.'

Hope walked to the door, opened it and was about to walk out when she turned her head to watch the man. He hit a putt and it sailed two inches to the left of the hole.

'You have to work out what you're doing and why it's going wrong. Otherwise, things don't change.' Before the man could answer, she shut the door hard behind her.

Chapter 15

Macleod sat outside on a wooden bench at motorway services just north of Glasgow. He sat looking at the piece of paper in front of him with the address for where the knives were dropped. The address given was Dunkeld, just north of Perth, and by routing to the north of Glasgow, the little green car was well on its way when Macleod wanted to stop and have a think about the address he'd been given. Clarissa was only too happy to pull over and try to find a coffee. However, it was the services, so Macleod was not hopeful on the quality of the beverage. It was a grey day, cool, but at least it wasn't raining. However, looking up at the clouds, it may not have been that far away.

The services were reasonably busy, being later in the day. Around Macleod were not just workmen heading home, but travellers ready to stop off at the roadside beds that were now provided at services. In the old days, it would have been hotels. Not now, everything was budget. Pop in, find a bed, on your way. *Maybe it was better*, thought Macleod. *After all, these were just functional places. It wasn't like it was a holiday for most people.*

They could be up at Dunkeld in an hour or so, but Macleod wanted to know if it was wise to investigate, wise to just approach this address. He didn't trust the niece or Gleary, although he'd stood and watched as Gleary had beat it out of her and then given her some extra. He wasn't sure, a lingering doubt in the back of his mind. If she'd been able to trade while keeping Gleary at a distance, just how good was she? Was she giving him an address to fob him off with?

Gleary wasn't a man you fobbed off lightly. He had been responsible for the deaths of many competitors. Macleod had never managed to nail him for it but he'd nailed many of his henchmen. He'd put people behind bars that made Gleary hate him, but never had he been able to implicate Gleary directly. The man was too wise for that. Nothing was ever in writing. Those who could have told you, who could have testified that Gleary gave the command, never would, fearing they'd end up inside a wooden box themselves.

He had tried hard to shut him down. The organised crime division worked hard at it too, but Macleod only ever got called in when there was a murder. Three occasions, Gleary had been inside the dock and every time they could never get him. Twice, they'd got his henchman, people who were so close to him, Gleary almost considered them sons. The other time it had all fallen apart. Macleod had thought it had been an inside job to wreck it, but those were Glasgow days.

Days that were now beyond him, his time now spent up in Inverness, away from the likes of Gleary, and he didn't want to go back to them. The man had clearly made peace that Macleod had moved on, and wasn't ready to hassle him again. Macleod was okay with that, though he hoped somebody at some point would bust the man wide open.

'Here's your coffee, Seoras. It's rubbish. Before you tell me.'
'Is it hot?'

'Should be. I saw the steam come off it.'

'Then it'll do. Did you have any trouble back at Gleary's?'

'No,' said Clarissa. 'Got a couple of magazines out. Had a bit of a chat.'

'Anyone threaten you?'

'No.'

'Well, at least I've still got some fear factor. Not a nice piece of work. He beat the girl we went to see, his own niece, smacked her about, as she wouldn't give him a proper answer. I knew he'd take out other people, but family? I suspect if she wasn't family, she'd probably be the next case up for the Glasgow Murder Team.'

'You move in such delightful circles, and you can't even tell anybody about this one.'

'What do you think about the address?' asked Macleod.

'Well, it makes sense,' said Clarissa. 'Travelling north and south, good place to drop things off. I mean, most of the murders have taken place at Inverness, but we've got our man in the borders. Easy place to come and pick your stuff up. I mean Dunkeld—who stops off at Dunkeld? You might stop off in Perth, but you don't really go through Dunkeld, do you?'

'Thought there was some sort of exhibition there. Beatrix Potter, is that not right?'

'Don't ask me. I'm an art collector, not a kids' book enthusiast.'

Macleod shook his shoulders. 'Well, question is, how much do we trust this information?'

'Thought you said he beat it out of her.' said Clarissa. 'I mean, if it's taken that much to take it out of her.'

'Wait,' said Macleod. 'That's the thing. Some of these people they'll hold, and they'll make it look like you've knocked it out of them. They're not daft. If she's pulling the blind over Gleary's eyes, she's going to be clever. She's going to be almost psychopathic. Let herself get beat to a pulp before allegedly giving out an address. Didn't sound like there were too many favours being done. I think Gleary just let this go because he didn't see the point of the knives. He's angry now though. Angry because kids are dying.'

'It's great to see some people have standards though, isn't it?' said Clarissa. 'Yes, if adults get knocked off, who cares? but the kids—No!'

'There's no real need for that tone,' said Macleod. 'You understand these guys have got a code. The way they work, they don't see it as doing something wrong. A lot of it's just business getting in the way of business. Usually, unless you're a bent cop or they don't do anything with you, they'll avoid you. Keep away.'

'They ever come after you?'

'I think there was once.' said Macleod. 'Once somebody had a go at me. I'm not sure Gleary ordered it though.'

'What happened?'

Macleod smiled. 'He stepped out of the door, managed to fall over my feet because for some reason I was standing waiting at the door. His nose hit the floor, smashed up and I put my knee in his back. A gun had fallen from his hand. You see, it's almost like I was prepared. Trouble was he threatened me. Gleary doesn't do that. That's why I think the guy did it without Gleary. Gleary would just kill you.'

'But what about the address?' asked Clarissa. 'As much as I'm enjoying this reminiscence.'

'Do we have an option? Is there any way we can get this place searched with anyone else? We can't really call Hope down to it. She can't race all the way down to Dunkeld without a solid reason.'

'Why not? Let me ring up.'

Macleod sipped his coffee while Clarissa got hold of her phone and contacted Hope.

'Oh, it's about time you called,' said Hope, answering the call. 'Why, what's up?'

'Been a bit of a fracas up here. We went off to cover everyone and I got taken out, chucked for a swim in the River Ness. Ross managed to pull me out. Nathan Mackie died.'

There was a sombre mood on the call, until Macleod asked her, through Clarissa, what was happening with the case. 'Are you running after Mackie's killer?'

Hope explained about the row she'd had with the DCI, but she had taken on Nathan Mackie's case anyway, but only as a pretence to keep the investigation going. She was going to look further but she wasn't getting any help from the DCI.

'Is he being obstructive?' asked Macleod through Clarissa.

'Slack almost,' said Hope. 'I've also said that a source is telling me all these things, a source has had me investigating Nathan Mackie. I haven't said who the source is.'

'That's because he knows,' said Macleod to Clarissa. 'Tell her he knows. He must know.'

'We've got an address,' said Clarissa, 'for the knives. We're thinking about going to it but is there any way you could do it officially?'

'To do what? And keep my source quiet? That won't work. If we find something, what are we going to say? Oh yes. My source said, and here's my source. Oh look, it's an investigating duo who shouldn't be operating. When we stepped out on this path, you knew that wasn't going to work,' said Hope.

She was able to be a lot franker because she agreed with Macleod, the DCI must know. In truth, simply talking to Macleod was not a great offence. Getting caught operating without authorisation would be the real problem.

'That's probably true,' said Macleod taking the phone, 'but this is what it is. Until we can get somewhere, and I can get myself reinstated, we must work it like this. What do you make of the address?'

'Who's it from?'

'Gleary. Well, Gleary's niece. I went through Gleary because they said that he was moving the package, but he wasn't. He approved it or gave the nod, but his niece was moving it. We went to see her. Very strange. We've got upside-down crosses and all sorts in the top flat she was in, and she runs a lot of drugs for Gleary. Got the feeling he wasn't too impressed with her on this one though. She wouldn't give an address out. Wouldn't say where the package had gone. He beat it out of her.'

'He did it in front of you?' asked Hope.

'Yes, and in front of me he knows that I'd have to open up about the acting without the due authority and that. Told me to keep my nose out though when I objected.'

'You did, didn't you?'

'I've nowhere to stand, but I played him right. I knew he wouldn't like the kids being killed. He's old school like that.'

'True. It's what they always said. I don't see we have many options, Seoras. You and Clarissa are going to have to go and look.'

'And what if we find things? We're going to have to stay on the outside. You're going to have to see where it goes. You're going to have to prove the links. You're going to have to go above the DCI. Can't you talk to Jim? Talk to the Assistant Chief Constable?'

'Not unless I've got something. Not unless I can show the DCI's involvement.'

'What's your take on him? What are you thinking, Hope? Is he involved in this or is he just slacking, protecting his backside? He was the one who made the call on Ian Lamb and then the guy killed himself. That's more than a lot of egg on your face. That can come back to haunt you.'

'I've got nothing at the moment,' said Hope. 'Nothing to turn around and say that he's manipulating this. He just seems to be standoffish. Just seems to not want to take anything in.'

'Of course, he doesn't. He sold me out in front of a TV crew. If this comes back, they'll be hounding for him. I do have a few supporters out there. I did until this was thrown up.

'Maybe that's the way to play it. Maybe that's what we need, Seoras, but you'll have to go to the house.'

'Okay but I think we'll scout it, not raid it. We'll leave it there, whatever we find. We need to try and get more on the group.

'Agreed,' said Hope. 'Completely. We don't know what we're dealing with here. What have we got with regards to the group? One dead body. Looks like Nathan Mackie slept with his own sister. Killed what would be his niece.'

'You need to not get on the wrong side of the DCI in case he's a player in the investigation,' said Macleod. 'I know it's probably winding you up. I know he's all over you. He's probably trying to set you up to be his sidekick, to be the go-to girl down below.'

'He's been asking me about being DI, says you're out of the picture now. I'm going to take over.'

'You have a good image though,' said Macleod. 'Physically.'

'Get out of it,' said Hope, realising he was winding her up, 'but there is that side too,' said Hope. 'Several times he's talked to me about how I wear my hair.'

'He never talked about mine,' said Macleod, laughing.

'Seriously though, Seoras, if I actually didn't know better and went down his line, I wonder where, how far he would go or what he would be interested in?'

'Let's not find that out. Sounds to me like he just wants to brush everything under the carpet. Has he not asked to bring anybody else in?'

'No, he was happy to leave Ross handling everything. Ross is good, but that's not what he needs to be doing. He's not got the authority to run a murder investigation on Nathan Mackie. All this DCI wants is reports, reports, reports. Then he drops in and ticks you off.'

'Stay with it and calm down. We'll let you know what we find out. Where are you going to start off with regards to Mackie?'

'Spoke to Ross. Apparently, he wants to go and see Jona. That's probably going to be our best bet. Forensics have been all over Ness Island to see if we can find any DNA or anything to link to the men who were there.'

'That's not going to work well is it? Anything you find in Ness Island could be from anywhere.'

'No big proof,' said Hope, 'but we might be able to pull a few names out of the hat. A few other people we could look at.'

'Okay,' said Macleod. 'Take care. You told Clarissa and she went off running like wildfire and now you've . . .'

'Stop! I know what I did, and I know why I did it and I was probably too quick. You don't need to lecture me.'

'I can't lecture you,' said Macleod. 'I'm not your boss anymore. I'm just an interested party. A common man right here in the bad, bad world of investigation.'

'Yes, it's nice having the shackles off, running things my way.'

Macleod laughed again. 'Take care, Hope,' he said. 'I know we always deal with murderers, but this feels different. These people feel extreme. Very extreme.'

'You too, Seoras. Can't be losing you either.'

'I'm the only one that hasn't gone into the middle of something,' he said. 'I got stitched up by my own DCI. No more murders.'

'There is time,' said Hope. 'There's always time.'

'Speak soon.' Macleod put the phone down, handed it back to Clarissa.

'You feel better for that?' she asked. 'That's the first time you've spoke to Hope in ages.'

'People don't get it,' said Macleod. 'They always look at the person in charge, the person running investigations. We're a team. As before, we're a team, but me and Hope especially. We're more of a team than anybody realises. I feel like I got my right hand back even if I'm no longer her boss.'

Chapter 16

Hope McGrath parked her car at the police station and walked slowly round to the forensic department where she would meet Ross and Jona Nakamura. She hadn't managed to reply to Jona when she was in the hospital, but there'd been several texts sent. The pair had shared an accommodation together before Hope had moved in with John, and they were as close as sisters. Hope always felt Jona had felt hurt when she'd had moved out, and although she was happy for her, she knew Jona missed her. She missed Jona, too, as she was fun and yet very incisive and had a way of thinking that rivalled Macleod.

She cut such a funny look with Hope as well, being so much smaller. On the few nights they'd been out, a couple of guys had commented on how Hope was the giant and Jona was the munchkin. The woman had the repartee to deal with that and had sent several of the guys packing, causing Hope simply to laugh watching them. She was also quite brilliant in the forensic lab and Hope knew she was dependent on Jona's team coming up with something from the murder scene of Nathan Mackie.

As she approached the door of the forensic lab, she saw Ross standing outside. He had his hands in his pockets and his head down but as she approached, he turned and smiled broadly.

'You still feel okay?' he asked.

'You didn't have to wait for me before I went in. You're allowed to go ahead of me.'

'I would never go in front of Macleod,' he said. 'He's the boss. You don't take the boss's thunder from him. Not if Jona is going to tell him something.'

'We don't even think like that. You do realise, don't you?'

'It's not right though,' said Ross. 'You don't do that to whoever's in charge. You let them find out the big things.'

'Have we got something big to find out?'

'I have no idea,' he said, 'but if there is, you'll find it out first.'

Hope walked past him, trying not to shake her head in disbelief. Ross was funny. He had his ways, very compartmentalised in the way he dealt with the world. Hope was certainly much more happy-go-lucky.

She opened the door of the forensic lab, stepped across, and asked one of the people inside where Jona was. She heard a shout, and then from behind several desks, she saw the short Asian woman make her way towards her. She was almost in a run, and as she reached Hope she flung her arms around her, holding her tight, her head barely making it halfway up from her waist.

'You're all right,' she said. 'Thank God, you're all right.'

'You should give Ross that hug, he's the one that deserves it. He's the one that kept me alive.'

Jona broke off her hug, walked up to throw her arms around Ross, but then held out her hand.

Ross shook it very politely. 'Thank you,' he said, 'but it's what anybody would do.'

129

'But you did it,' said Jona. 'You did it and I've still got my friend.'

As she turned back, Hope thought she could see tears in Jona's eyes, but by the time they'd walked over to her desk, she'd wiped them clean and she was the professional once again.

'How're we doing?' asked Hope.

'Well,' said Jona, 'it's quite a big site. You've got a lot of flowing water and it rained last night, which didn't help. We found a couple of footprints which we're taking casts of, trying to see if we can match them up with anyone, but I'm not sure we will. We don't know who we're looking for, after all.'

'No, we don't. Anything else though?'

'I've had a couple of strands of hair from Nathan.' She pointed over towards a Petri dish, pulling it towards her. 'Expecting the DNA analysis back on it anytime, but we're not sure if it's going to yield anything. Outside of that, we're really struggling. We found a couple of gloves, but they look like kids' gloves. I'm not even sure they're involved. This is such a busy part of Inverness, people wandering round; you find these footprints here and there. We're going to struggle, and even if we do find a footprint, you haven't given me any sizes or suspects to link it to. Going to be very difficult.'

'Appreciate that,' said Hope, 'but was kind of hoping you would come up with something because we're stuck.'

Jona leaned in closely to her. 'Is there anything else coming through? Any other sources?'

Hope closed in as well. 'We're still tracing the knives. We've got an address and some of our friends are going to check it out. If we find them, we'll have to work the best way to get them into your hands. They can't just appear.'

'No, they can't. Let's see what you can do. Sometimes things get posted anonymously,' said Jona. 'It's sort of a conscience thing. You've got a man who's dead now. He might have a conscience. Might have sent it before.'

'Well, pick it up from the post,' said Hope, 'but the date would be wrong. Be after he died.'

'We can work that out,' said Jona.

Hope looked a little shocked, but if that was what it took to get this investigation back on track, maybe it was worth doing. Jona turned away to discuss something with a colleague and then said she'd be back shortly with some results. Hope stood, looking around the forensic lab with the industrious busy bees around her and then saw Ross looking at her.

'What?' she said.

'I don't like this. I don't like this disorder. I don't like working in the dark. I don't like being dumped on having to fight to save you. This is wrong. We shouldn't be operating like this. I should go and see the DCI, sort it.'

'No,' said Hope. 'No, you don't. I like you, Alan, I really do. I depend on you; so did Macleod, but that's not your forte. These guys, they would prey on your decency, your honesty, and you couldn't screw them over quick enough before they would take you over a barrel. Leave the DCI to me.' She realised she'd put her hands on her hips, almost giving a Wonder Woman pose, but Ross had the decency not to mention it.

'If that's what you want, that's what I'll do.'

'Good,' she said, and looked around for Jona who hadn't returned. 'What's going on with the adoption procedures though?' asked Hope.

'Still unclear. They leave you waiting a lot. They'll make their decision, this and that. I mean, you get quicker decisions on the telly with that dancing thing. At least they only leave you hanging for twenty-four hours.'

'True,' said Hope. 'There's been a lot on your mind though, especially with everything else.'

'I'm trying to get a child. Well, we are,' said Ross. 'It's not like I've lost my career. It's not like I've been accused of being sloppy, leading to children dying. I think the boss is having it worse.'

'Don't you worry about the boss. I think you'll find the boss is a little bit more ready to work outside the law than you think. We'll see what happens when they go to Dunkeld. Hopefully, they'll come back with something for us, because it looks like we're out of luck with Jona.'

It was then the woman burst in through the door, making her way directly to them. The Asian gave a smile and threw a bit of paper down on the table.

'What's that?' asked Hope.

'That's a piece of paper that says that the hair that was in Nathan's hands has very similar DNA as Nathan Mackie who happens to have same DNA that we found on his sister. I don't know whose hair this is. Do you think it could be Kyle's?'

Hope looked at the few strands that were in the Petri dish.

'Can you take that colour and make it into hair colour?' asked Ross. 'I mean produce a wig from it, multiple strands so we see the colour a person would be looking at. See if we have some idea of whose head it is. I mean, I know it won't be accurate, but it might at least give us the hair colour of the individual.'

'Just a moment,' said Jona. The Petri dish was under a microscope that was attached to a computer. It took a few minutes before she threw up a head of hair on a 3D rendering face.

132

'That looks like nobody we know,' said Hope.

'You're wrong there,' said Ross. 'Don't look at the shape of the hair. Don't look at the face. Just the colour. Whose hair is that colour? He had a hat on last time. Not easy to see. Not easy to remember.'

'The DNA is similar,' said Hope, 'because it's his brother.'

'Well, it certainly looks like it, doesn't it?'

'I think we need to find out when he last saw his brother. We don't tell him about this though,' said Hope. 'I don't think he'll throw in, 'Oh by the way, he ruffled his hands through my hair,' for us. He said he hadn't seen him for weeks or longer. This will prove he's lying. One of the group.'

'So what? He just came along and killed his brother?' asked Jona.

'He's probably in the group. He's let the family down. He's let the group down. I mean, Nathan's possibly gone to bed with his sister. His brother's probably very annoyed at that. I mean, why? What's that all about?'

'I don't get it,' said Ross. 'I don't get the way he is or rather the way he was.'

'Nonetheless, it's a good reason to go to them. Good reason to visit. Probably be able to pull him in as well.'

'It's a good call,' said Ross. 'Thank you, Jona.'

'It's a bit much though,' said Hope. 'To go and kill your brother if the other one had been with his sister. We don't know enough about this family. We don't know enough background.'

'He may also go on the run though,' said Ross. 'Think about it. If he just killed his brother, nothing to stop him disappearing off, is there?'

'Except that would look suspicious. What have we got at the

moment? There's been no more child killings. We've got the body of Nathan Mackie. They don't know I've got his hair. They don't know that we might be onto them. I think the best thing to do, Ross, is to go and tackle him, talk to him, see where he's been. Let him put down a whole history that we can blow apart. Then I might be able to pull him in properly, interview him.'

'That'll be enough to put suspicion on him and we'll be able to tail him. Bring in more than ourselves,' said Ross. 'Feels like we could do with a lot more than ourselves.'

'You also need to check through these footprints we're doing,' said Jona. 'We don't do this for the good of our health. If you can get his shoe size, maybe even some of his shoes, we'll be able to check it against the prints. Sounds like we might be getting somewhere though,' she said. 'Also understand, Nathan Mackie was a twin to Sandra. Their DNA is incredibly close. That's why we couldn't identify him. Though why he wanted to sleep with her, who knows?'

'Well, thanks, Jona,' said Hope, and she turned around, saying to Ross, 'I'm going to head back to the office.' As she went to leave, a hand grabbed hers.

'Stay a minute,' said Jona.

'I'll see you up top, Ross.'

Ross gave a nod and Hope turned back to Jona who'd pointed towards her office. Hope followed the Asian woman in. Once Jona closed the door behind her, she pulled down the curtain, reached forward with her hands and took Hope's.

'I thought I'd lost you,' she said. 'If it hadn't been for Ross.'

'Well, it was Ross. He was there and he did a good job of it, so let's not worry. I'm fine. Part and parcel of being an officer,' said Hope.

'No, it's not. You're swaggering in there as if nothing's wrong, but I can see the anger inside. What's happened?'

'DCI is playing us, messing us about here, there, and everywhere. Doesn't want us to go after anybody. Can't see that these killings are still linked into this group. Nathan Mackie was probably part of the group.'

'You haven't got any evidence, have you?' said Jona. 'What is coming in is coming in from the side. The best thing you can do is to be there before there's another one. Stop it. That will be your proof. That'll be proof that Seoras was not at fault. It would be hard for the DCI to keep a copycat thing going.'

'That's true,' said Hope. 'It'd be a comeback from the grave effort.'

'Have you spoken to Seoras?' said Jona quietly.

'Yes. Why?'

'Wondering how he's holding up.'

'He seems fine. I can't believe he's working so much of this on the outside, but I don't know where he's been driven from. Yes, he's had his name tarnished. Yes, there's kids involved, but he doesn't even seem to be caring about normal procedures. He had to go and watch a beating from one of our old foes back down south. The guy beat his niece to get an address for the boss. That's not Seoras.'

'You do understand about the symbols?'

'The symbols?' asked Hope. 'What do you mean? I mean, I know there's lots and lots of different cultures in this, tied into what this group believes.'

'No,' said Jona. 'I don't mean that. I mean with Seoras. You understand what the symbols do to him.'

'No, I'm not with you.'

'The thing about Seoras is that he always seems like he's

135

come to terms with his religion, and in some ways, he has. He's not that closed-minded person that used to live down in Glasgow. When we did our meditation together, he told me about how he used to feel, told me about how you had helped him come to terms to be a different person, to understand his faith more, to know its place in what he did, but this is affecting him.

'There's nothing he holds dearer than that faith in his heart. Not even Jane, not even his first wife. The moment there was an upside-down cross on the kid, it affected him. Just watch him on this one,' said Jona, 'and yourself, because he won't stop. Part of him will see this as God's work. Not just in the sense that we're up against something evil, in the sense that God himself is behind him.'

Hope nodded, thanked Jona, and hugged her. The two women held the embrace and Hope realised just how close her being to death had affected Jona, but when she closed the door and started to walk for the office, she realised that the whole case was affecting everyone in its own way. She charged in, so did Clarissa. Ross was struggling with the lack of coordination and how everything had been pulled apart, and Seoras—was he just trying to get his name back, or was this some sort of righteous quest as well?

Chapter 17

The little green sports car sped along north of Perth where before long, the A9 began to sweep in between small mountains, trees lining either side of the road of the single carriageway which slowed the traffic down somewhat. Macleod looked with a little consternation that Clarissa would speed out past someone and then back in.

'There's no need for that,' she said. 'You're technically not in the force, are you? You're suspended? Well, on gardening leave or whatever. You're allowed to speed.'

'But you're not,' he said. 'Just calm it down. We don't want anybody to spot who we are.'

'They're never going to spot you with that hoodie. It's so un-you, it's incredible.'

The day was coming towards evening. Macleod reckoned darkness would soon take over, but Clarissa made such good time that they arrived at Dunkeld while there was still good daylight. She turned off the A9, trying to follow the satnav to where the house was. It was outside the main village, and she went over a couple of bridges before arriving at a house set apart from the rest and hidden by a large number of trees.

'Certainly secluded. Good place to switch things up,' said

Clarissa.

'Just don't take the car all the way in,' said Macleod. 'Park a wee bit away from it out at the roadside.'

'You sure?' asked Clarissa. 'Could just pop on in.'

'No. You might want to put your hood up. I think the rain is coming soon.'

Macleod stood beside the car after she parked, hoodie over him like some sort of vagrant who was missing a bottle of whiskey. Clarissa, still sporting her tartan shawl but with a black pair of trousers, rubbed her hands, feeling the cold that was setting in.

'Watch my back when we go in here,' said Macleod. 'We want to look around, but we don't want to be unsafe. Too many things have happened of late. Let's just be careful.'

'I hear you,' said Clarissa, and took up a position about two feet behind Macleod as they walked. She kept checking behind her but Macleod was aware that the footsteps never drifted away.

As he approached the house, he walked up the small stony drive to where the two-floored building lay in amongst the trees. Slowly, he walked up and rapped the door, not knowing if he'd get an answer, but was prepared to use a story about breaking down, part of the reason of leaving the car further away.

'There's nothing doing,' said Clarissa when no one came to the door. 'Should I take a scout round the back?'

'*We* ought to take a look round the back. Don't go too far away. Keep each other within sight at all times.'

'Okay, Seoras, you're the boss.'

'Wasn't aware that I was,' he said absentmindedly, and proceeded to walk around the edge of the house. The house was fairly old. He placed it at maybe thirty or forty years, and every window had curtains drawn. Had they shut up shop and left? He didn't know so he walked around to the rear and tried the back door. It opened with ease.

'That's unusual,' he said. 'Stay at the door a minute.'

Macleod had entered into a kitchen with another door to the right. He opened it and peered in. There was a certain dampness to the place but the furniture looked relatively modern. There were some photos of children, but as much as he scanned around, he couldn't see two children who matched. Maybe they were cut out of magazines just to give the impression that there was a family here.

'Come on in with me,' he said, not wanting to go any further to leave Clarissa behind. He heard her boots tap as they marched across the kitchen floor and she followed him into the other room. It was a dining room with a simple wooden table, four chairs around it.

'It's like a family house,' said Clarissa.

'Very much so,' said Macleod, 'except for that far-right corner.'

Clarissa looked over, then tapped Macleod's shoulder. 'What's in the far-right corner?'

Macleod stopped, turned around, and walked over, bending down and picking up the remains of a roll-up.

'Family house where they just chuck the cigarettes in the corner. I don't think so,' he said. 'Stay close.'

Together, they edged through another door into the front living room. There was a large television in one corner which the sofa faced. They noticed a couple of bottles of alcohol, and not many of them were classy. Walking out of the other living room door, he saw the stairs as well as another door through to another front room. He opened it quickly. There was nothing there except a bed and a small dressing table. Macleod rifled through it but found nothing.

'I'll go upstairs,' he said, 'you stay at the bottom. Get out that door if I shout.'

Clarissa nodded and watched Macleod climb the stairs. When he was at the top, the man turned and signalled for her to come up to him, and only when she'd arrived, did they move forward.

In the first bedroom there was a large double bed, which was unkempt, covers thrown off, and some clothes lying around the floor. Macleod checked the wardrobes. There was nothing unusual. Just clothes, shoes.

They checked another two bedrooms and a bathroom, but again, nothing unusual. The two other bedrooms were kids' rooms with toys and photos up in the wall, but Macleod didn't recognise any of the kids in the photos from the photos downstairs.

Maybe they didn't need to. Maybe that was the point. Anybody else would come in and just look around. Macleod was looking for everything. Together, they slowly crept down the stairs and peered out of the windows. They could see no one.

'Well, if they've used it, it's a bust,' said Clarissa, 'because they're not using it now, or if they are, they're not here. Maybe they got wind. Maybe she told him.'

'It still would've been used,' said Macleod. 'I wonder . . .'

He made his way along the hall, turning into where the hangers for coats were. He looked down at the floor. It was wooden, with a rug over it. He reached down and pulled the rug back and found a trapdoor with a finger hole, allowing him to pull it up. He opened it, told Clarissa to wait at the top while he peered in with the light from his pocket torch.

When the beam shone around, he could see racks on which sat several packets of white powder. There were also other boxes down there.

'This could be it,' he said. 'We'll need to take a look down. It's going to leave us exposed at the top though. We can't throw that rug back over and close the lid.'

'Do you want me to stay up here?' asked Clarissa.

'No, I'm not sure that's going to be wise. Probably best if you get down here and we quickly search it and get back up. There's been nobody about. If we're quick, we can do this in a couple of minutes and get out.'

Clarissa nodded and followed Macleod down a set of concrete steps into the basement. He shone his torch around. There were racks, but certainly no windows down here. They wondered how the air flowed through, although it couldn't have flowed in much volume because it was as stale as could be. Macleod started rifling through the boxes that were on the racks. He pulled out some tablets thinking they were amphetamines, then tore open some more to find a white powder.

'Drugs,' he said. 'Why are they running drugs? Why would they take the knives on if this was their main business? She must have been making enough off of this. Why risk taking any knives on? How much money do you get paid for this compared to the knives? I don't like this,' he said. 'Something smells wrong about this.'

There was a sudden thud, and Macleod realised it was the trapdoor being closed. He turned and bolted for the stairs, shining the flashlight, but tripped on the first stairs, grazing his knee before pulling himself back up. As he got to the top, he found the trapdoor closed and he pushed at it, but it wouldn't move.

He could see the hole where his finger had gone through to pull up the trapdoor and there was light beyond. He heard a laugh and then something covered over the hole. He shone his torch up at it to see what it was, and saw a hose being put through. Suddenly, water splashed in his face as the hose was turned on.

'What's happening?' said Clarissa.

'They shut the trapdoor. They're starting to put water in,' said Macleod.

'What? They mean to drown us? They mean to trap us in here with the water?'

'I don't know,' said Macleod.

He stepped back down and started going around the walls with his torch. Everywhere he went he saw damp, but also solid, brick. They were under the ground, albeit just under the ground, but definitely not above the surface. He wondered how porous the walls were. Would they hold the water that was being poured in? It was coming fairly slowly, but that didn't matter over time if it kept filling up.

For the next ten minutes, Macleod started pushing here and there at the walls seeing if there was any weakness. He then reached up to the ceiling looking for any gaps up there, but there were beams across up onto solid floor. The wooden floor above was nailed down. His heart began to sink. His feet were now getting wet, the water level rising, and he thumped at the trapdoor.

'What do you want? Tell us what you want.'

There came no answer.

'Is there anywhere to turn water off?' asked Macleod. 'Do the pipes come through here? Is there anywhere we can break it open?'

Clarissa had her torch out as well and was scanning the sides. Macleod, as he walked past one packet of white powder, couldn't help himself but rip it open. He put his finger in and tested it.

'Flour,' he said. 'We're set up. This is flour.'

'There's pipes in the corner here,' said Clarissa. 'I don't know if we can break them though.'

Macleod looked around the room and then kicked over one of the racks that had been holding the white powder. He pulled at it, then jumped up and down on the corner before one of the main pillars of the rack started to come away. With Clarissa's help, he managed to get it clear.

'Start hitting the pipe. See if we can find a weakness in it.'

He started to thump it, hitting it as hard as he could and saw a small dent. 'More,' he said, 'more.'

For the next twenty minutes, Macleod battered it, but he felt his arms becoming tired. The pipe had started to move, started to indent, but it was slow work.

'Give me it, Seoras,' said Clarissa, 'give me it. Take a rest for a minute while I do this.'

Macleod went to sit down, but found himself having to go up at least three of the steps. The water was now up to their shins. He watched, sucking in breath, shining his torch on the pipe as Clarissa smacked it again and again. In fairness, he thought she hit it harder than he did. Then all of a sudden, the pipe split.

'I've got it,' she said, 'I've got it.'

Macleod looked up to the pipe coming in through the

trapdoor and grabbed a hold of it. He'd been unable to push it back up. Obviously, held down somewhere above, but now he saw the water reduced to a trickle.

'You've done it,' he said. 'You've done it. The water, it's stopping.'

'It's pissing out here,' said Clarissa. 'We've just busted where it's coming out of. Instead of coming out of the pipe through the hole, it's coming out of here. Quick. Get your hands on this.'

Macleod ran over, but the pipe had weakened. All of a sudden, it split completely and the water was pouring out.

'Can we stuff it?' asked Macleod.

Clarissa tried to, but the pressure was too great. The water just kept coming. She took off her shawl and began to shove it up the pipe, but again, the water pressure just pushed it back out.

'Now, Seoras, what do we do? What do we do?'

The next hour was spent trying to re-cover the pipe. There wasn't much there with which to block it, and every bit of paper, cardboard, or fabric that was shoved up it ended up being forced back out again. An hour and a half later, Macleod and Clarissa were sitting on the top three steps of a flooded basement.

'What can we do?' she said. 'What can we do?' Macleod was trying to heave up the trapdoor, but nothing was happening.

'I don't know,' said Macleod, 'I can't see any other way out.'

'Start shouting,' said Clarissa, 'it's the only thing we've got.' She began to scream at the top of her voice so hard that it hurt Macleod's ears. 'It's the only thing we've got.' The water, over the next five minutes, rose again.

'Seoras, I'm scared. Seoras, what the hell do we do? What

do we damn well do?'

Macleod was lost for words. He'd now had to tilt his neck back. The water was in his ears, and he just about kept his mouth and nose above it, but his nose was touching the trapdoor above. He reckoned they had another five minutes at most. He could feel her shaking, feel her panic. In truth, he thought this was it.

Chapter 18

Hope and Ross drove straight to the home of Kyle Mackie, arriving as the sky began to get dark. Ross wondered if anyone would be inside tonight. Would a mysterious woman visit with a bottle of wine again, presumably to then stay the night? As they parked up, they could see the window of the man's house and he sat in the kitchen eating what was his dinncr.

Hope felt somewhat famished and grabbed a small snack bar as she left the car, polishing it off and putting the wrapper in her back pocket. She felt like she'd been on the go constantly, despite only just coming out of the hospital that morning. Both Macleod and Clarissa were on the go too. Everyone was. It was a case of all hands to the oars, and to see how far they could drive this ship, see if they could steer a course to some sort of solution. To possibly some sort of evidence that they could take to the DCI to cause more investigation.

Hope was sure that there was a significant group behind what was going on, a good number of people, and she didn't believe that it was a case of just one person committing these acts. Somebody like Ian Lamb had been a very convenient sacrifice.

Hope marched up to the door, banged on it, and stood back waiting for the arrival of Kyle Mackie. As he opened the door, she smiled openly, unnerving the man.

'Mr. Mackie, sorry to have come with some disturbing news for you.'

'What's that?' he asked.

'Your brother Nathan. I'm afraid he has been murdered.'

'Murdered?' said the man. 'Doesn't surprise me. What did Nathan get himself into this time? I told you we don't bother with each other. It's no real skin off my nose.'

'When did you last see your brother?' asked Hope.

'Some time ago. We don't tend to keep close contact. He's not my favourite. Neither is Sandra. Wasn't a great family, sergeant, not a great family to grow up in. Thank you for the news.'

'If I could just stop you a moment,' said Hope as the man went to close the door. 'I've got a few further questions. Would you mind if I came in?'

'Is your friend coming as well? Only, he was outside the other night keeping an eye on me. Put off my lady friend.'

'Which lady friend was that?' asked Hope.

'Just a lady friend I have.'

'What's her name?' asked Ross. 'I didn't catch you from outside and in case you were wondering, we were just making sure you were okay. We knew your brother was under threat, or at least one of you was.'

Hope wished he hadn't said that. Maybe the man would link things and would see that they were fishing for a reason to bring him in.

'What's her name?' asked Ross again.

'Anna. Anna is a Polish migrant. She sometimes does a bit

of cleaning for me, but she's quite tolerable, pleasant on the eye. I invited her along to see if she would want to become my assistant.'

'Do the assistant's duties take place upstairs?' asked Ross.

'Things developed. It's not my place to stop things developing, is it? I mean, she's at liberty to sleep with me, as much as anybody else.'

'She brought a bottle of wine with her,' said Ross. 'Looks like it was probably a bit more of a planned move rather than accidentally finding you incredibly attractive.'

Hope glanced at Ross. He was being sarky. He needed to be careful because he could push the man. Hope wanted to nail him, wanted to trap him. His hair was on his brother's body, clutched in the hands.

'I need to ask you,' said Hope, 'would you mind doing a DNA test?'

'Why would I do a DNA test? Why would I submit to that? Am I some sort of suspect?'

'No. No, not at all,' said Hope. 'One of the reasons is that we would look to eliminate you from inquiries. Your name's come up. Quite frankly, it's probably nothing. In fact, we believe you probably were more the victim than anything, but we just need to be careful. If you did a DNA test for us, we'd speed up the process. We could eliminate you very easily. I wonder if you'd be up for that.'

The man walked back to his dinner that was sitting on the kitchen table, picked up a sausage on a fork, and bit into it. He chewed it over and Hope could see him thinking.

'What'd you say?' asked Hope. 'You going to do it for me? It'll be a big help, sir.'

'You've nothing to fear,' said Ross. 'After all, you haven't seen your brother, or you haven't been about him. There's not going to be a problem, is there?'

Once again, the man returned to his food, leaving the two officers standing there while he chewed thoughtfully.

'Well, obviously there's nothing for me to worry about, but tell me how he died?'

'Your brother?' said Ross, making the point that there had been a long time since they were on that part of the conversation. 'Unfortunately, he was attacked on the islands in the River Ness. Badly mutilated, not in a very good way.'

'One would wonder how it'd be a good way to die in any particular way,' said the man. 'Nathan was always the dark horse of the family though, getting himself into things. Sad really; we all get the same genes, don't we, or near enough with siblings? Some of us just make more of them. Look at Sandra.'

'Well, if we could just take a swab from your mouth, that would be great,' said Hope, 'We'd have your DNA then.'

'Just a moment. In fact, if you just follow me through here,' said the man stepping out of the kitchen and Hope followed him quickly. He moved with an ease, fast, but as though he wasn't trying.

'Stay here,' said Hope to Ross and quickly followed the man through the kitchen door. She saw another door open farther down the hall, but by the time she got through it, she was entering what looked like an empty room. She thought she heard a large box at the end, close.

The room she was in was covered with items from a magician's treasure trove. She saw a little guillotine, glanced at the box that got sawn in two. There was a dunk tank as well. But straight ahead of her was a large box with a gaping hole underneath. The doors of course had just shut. Hope reached forward, pulling them open, but no one was inside. She raced around the side again, pulling the others open until eventually she could see right through.

'Ross,' she shouted, 'Ross, get outside, cover the exits.'

'What's the matter?'

'He's just vanished. He's just damn well vanished.'

Hope began tearing around the room, pulling out cupboards, and shifting some equipment back to see if there were holes in the wall. But the man was gone.

After she checked each of the four walls and the floor and the ceiling, she raced outside looking for Ross. The house was semi-detached and the house beside still had lights on so Hope ran over and knocked on the door quickly. A woman answered.

'Detective Sergeant Hope McGrath. I need to enter your house now and search.'

'Search? Why do you need to search? Have you got some warrant to search? What's wrong? Why are you looking at me? I haven't done anything.'

'No, you haven't. You've done nothing, but I believe the man next door might be in your house.'

'What? What do you mean the man next door is in my house? Is he spying? Is it some peephole thing?'

Hope didn't have time for this, but she couldn't very well just barge into someone's house either. 'I'm sorry, but I need to check the inside of your house.'

'You need to explain it to me,' said the woman. Hope pushed on through. She looked inside a living room, dining room, and a kitchen before rushing upstairs, checking all the bedrooms to see no one there. She bolted back down and out through the front door with the bewildered woman looking at her.

Hope picked up her phone. 'Ross, have you found him? Is he about?'

'I've searched around the back. I can't see anything. His car's still there.'

Hope checked the drive and confirmed with Ross that the car was still there.

'How the hell's he done this?' asked Hope. 'Damn, we'll need him. He's the link to the group. He's the . . .'

'I'm still searching around the back,' said Ross. 'I can't see him anywhere. He's gone. How did he leave the room?'

The room thought Hope. *That's it. The room.* She raced back inside the house into the magic room and began searching again. She checked the floor but could find nothing. There was a carpet throughout and you would have to pull up most of it just to get through it, and under the floor. None of the walls gave any secret passage. She could find no lines or gaps. She checked all the equipment, all the boxes opened but Kyle Mackie was not inside.

Then she looked up at the ceiling again. She scanned it with her eyes, but it was beyond even her height to touch it without any help. She ran into the kitchen and pulled through a chair and started pushing up at the ceiling here, there and everywhere, until finally one patch seemed to open. Hope picked up her phone again.

'Ross, I know how he did it. He's gone upstairs. I'm going to wait down here by the stairs until you get back. Okay? Hurry.'

Hope walked out of the room and manned the staircase, in case anyone ran down from above. Ross arrived panting, his tie over his shoulder.

'You stay there. I'm going to go up to the bedrooms.'

'Just be careful,' said Ross. 'Surely better if I go up the stairs as well.'

'Good idea,' said Hope, and she raced back through into the magician's rear room. Quickly she stood on the stool, pushed, and opened the trap door in the ceiling she'd found, and then hauled herself up. As her hair appeared through the top, she looked around but saw nobody but Ross. There was an open window in the room. The bed sheets were tied together, hung out of the window and as Hope made it up and over to the window, she heard the starting of a car.

'Quick, downstairs,' she shouted and the pair of them legged it as quick as they could. By the time they got outside, the car was gone.

'Tell me you clocked the license plate,' said Hope. 'Please, Ross, tell me.'

Ross rhymed off the license without even thinking.

'Phone it in,' said Hope. 'I want that car found.'

'DCI's not going to like that.'

'Hell with the DCI. Just get on with it, Ross.' She glanced over and saw the man tapping into the phone, but his eyes were cold. She'd been too brutal. Too quick to snap at him.

Damn it, she thought. *How had she been fooled? Bloody magicians. They seriously had this set up?*

Once Ross had phoned the licence number through, Hope returned to search the main room where all of the equipment was. She pulled out every item stored in every box, not being too careful, but also not wanting to screw about too much. Jona would have to come in, but there needed to be something. The man had to leave in a hurry. He didn't know they were coming, so maybe he'd made a mistake. Maybe something was around.

'They'll be out here shortly, Boss. Anything I can do?' Ross asked Hope.

'Go through these boxes, drawers, anything. See if there's anything about.'

Hope could feel the sweat on her face, the adrenaline pounding through her body. They'd been caught out. If they'd had a proper contingent, they could have encircled the house. He never would've got away if she hadn't called Ross back in. He was right, of course, going for the pincer movement. Then the man had popped outside.

Jona would get her DNA though, surely that wouldn't be a problem. There'd be enough things in the house for that. That's why he'd run. He must have reckoned they had something, something that would tie him to the murders, and he was probably right.

She pulled open the bottom drawer on a large oak table. Hope saw a piece of paper, A4 in size with lots of symbols on it. There was at least twenty-odd lines, all in their symbology, this picture language.

'Something there?' asked Ross, seeing how keen she was on looking at it. Hope put it out before her and tried to read what was said there. The paper was all just symbols, just gibberish with nothing to indicate what any symbols meant.

Clarissa had been the one on the symbols. She'd gone and got a professor to look at them and Hope needed somebody to translate. She picked up the phone, dialled a number and realised that she couldn't get through. There was no signal where Seoras and Clarissa were now; after all, they were heading for Dunkeld, weren't they?

Hope thought they might be out of there by now. Maybe they were heading up towards Inverness. You did lose the signal several times on the way up although in fairness, there were now more mobile masts along the A9, and the situation was better than it had been. Hope put the phone away.

'Remind me, Ross,' she said, 'to give the boss and Clarissa a ring in a couple of hours. Sounds like they're incommunicado at the moment. I can't seem to get through.'

'I'll make sure we get everything bagged and tagged,' said Ross.

'Flip, Ross, we had him. You and I had him and he just pulls some sort of illusion on me.'

'We all get burnt,' said Ross. 'We all get played. Even the boss.'

Chapter 19

The water was rising still, and Macleod was doing his best to float on his back, but it was so close now to the ceiling of the room that he was hanging onto the trapdoor mounts with his hands. Clarissa was in a similar position, her shawl now discarded, and Macleod thought she wasn't remaining as calm as he was. He knew death would come.

At some point, he would end in this life, but he had no fear of the next part of the journey as they called it. He was out fighting the fight. This was a cause most worthy and in fact, due to the devil worship that appeared to be involved, he considered it to be a fight he was obliged to be in. One that was beyond mere police work.

He didn't think anyone else would see it like that. Maybe Jane. The others would see Macleod coming back to be the police officer he once was. This was more than that. That was why he could reach out to Gleary, the gang lord. Why he could go down these other paths that were not good. *God bless Clarissa*, he thought. She had gone through it all with him.

'Seoras, can I tell you something?'

His hand reached out and touched Clarissa's.

'There's no time. So . . .'

'We'll be okay. Stay calm.'

'I can't stay calm,' she said. 'My nose is touching the ceiling. We've maybe got five or ten minutes at most. No one's coming.'

'Of course, someone will come. We'll get there.'

'Seoras, you daft bugger. Nobody's coming for us. This is it. This is you and me. This is how it ends.'

Macleod worked his hand around to find the hose that had been in the room. He previously tried to push it back up, but there'd been somebody there holding It in position. But now as he pushed back, there was no one.

'Clarissa, the hose is moving. The hose is moving. We need to keep going with it. Keep pushing.'

'If I move from here', she said, 'I'll not get back. I'm just about above the water.'

'Then I'll get it,' he said.

IIer words were coming to him through the water where his ears were now covered. But he closed his eyes briefly and pushed himself down into the water before turning around. It was dark and he grasped the hose by feel before pushing it backward.

He kept going on and on and then put a hand out, feeling where Clarissa was. Once he grabbed her hand, he pushed himself up, desperate for a breath, and smacked his head off the ceiling. Ignoring the pain, he reached up with his lips, and broke clear. Quickly, he sucked in some air.

He went further down, again kept pushing the hose back, feeling what seemed like an endless loop until he found the start of it. He continued after two more breaths until the hose was right up against the ceiling where the trap door was. With two fingers, he pushed the edge of it out, up through the trap door. There was little room left, but now there was another supply of air in.

He pushed his hand out to the trap door, feeling for the gap which was there. He pushed as hard as he could with his hand, and although it wasn't much of an effort, due to the fact he was trapped in the water, he managed to raise it slightly only for it to come back down.

'They put something on top of it,' he said, his fist pressed up to the ceiling.

'What did you say?' asked Clarissa.

'They've put something on top of it. I can't shift it; give me your hand.'

He took Clarissa's hand, put it under the trap door beside his hand.

'Now push,' he said, 'push as hard as you can.'

The trap door lifted, maybe by an inch, maybe two, and then it fell hard back down on top of them.

'The swine,' said Clarissa. 'Damn it,' and then he heard a gulp. She'd sunk down under the water and taken in some. He reached for her, lifting her shoulders up pressing her head upwards until it touched the ceiling. He could hear a choke, but then she was breathing again, rasping, fighting to get rid of the water she'd swallowed.

'Take it easy, easy, slowly,' he said. 'Nice and easy, then we can try again, see if we can shift it, push in a burst.'

'Seoras,' she said, 'I don't know how much longer I can keep this up.'

'All day,' he said. 'You can keep it all day; you're my Rottweiler; you can take them all on—you know that.'

'Jane didn't deserve you.'

'What?' asked Macleod.

'She didn't deserve you; you needed somebody alongside you like a fighter, somebody that understood the job.'

'Like who?' asked Macleod, and then there was silence. The silence grew until it was interrupted by a choky splutter.

'There's no point going there,' said Macleod. He didn't have the heart to tell her that he wouldn't have been interested. He liked her well enough as a person; she was a good detective, if somewhat abrasive, but she wasn't what he would need or someone he could really give to.

'Been a long time since, well, I had someone, and then you had to walk in, didn't you?' she muttered. 'Walk in attached, story of my damn life. What'd I get to do? I get to die with you.'

'We're not going to die,' said Macleod. 'We're going to be okay because someone's going to come, we're going to push this away; now, shut up and give me a hand.'

'Listen to you, you don't even believe what you've said, I can tell.'

'I should have brought Hope,' said Macleod suddenly.

He heard Clarissa laugh and then she choked again on some water as it managed to get inside her mouth. 'Don't, don't make jokes,' she said. 'Don't. Stop it, I can't, I can't.'

'We need to push this up,' said Macleod. 'Now, give me a hand.'

He felt her cling on to his, as they scrabbled in the dark for the trapdoor. He pushed her hand up to where the trap door was, his beside hers, and told her to push the trap door.

'Lift it up. Maybe an inch. Push it hard, ram it. Hit it again, again,' he said excitedly. It maybe lifted three inches before whatever was on top slammed it back down.

'So, it's useless,' said Clarissa. 'It's useless.'

'It's never useless. It's never useless to fight,' he said. 'You're a fighter. Come on.'

'I don't want to have my last moments spent fighting. I want some rest. I've never had rest. Do you understand that? You're not feeling that, getting older? You power off.'

Oh, he did. He'd almost been at peace, at peace to slip off into retirement. Take Jane and disappear. Stuff the record, stuff what they thought of him. Then Clarissa had walked in, given him a kick up the backside, rallied him, and now she needed him. Needed him to rally her.

'I could just let go,' she said. 'Just drift off.'

'No, you won't, Sergeant. You're a detective sergeant. You're here to fight. You'll fight for those kids, like you told me to come and fight.'

He heard her laugh again. 'It's a good run though,' she said. 'I never thought I'd be in the murder squad. What made you put me in the murder squad? You don't get stuff like this in the art world. You get to spot forgeries; you get to see who's nicked what. You get elaborate plots that fool insurance companies. We don't get this, getting drowned in a cellar. You never warned me about this, Seoras. You never said to me, 'Oh by the way, just be fully aware that you can get into some serious trouble here. You might have to entertain a dying DI. Pretend everything's all right.'

'That's enough,' he said. 'That's enough.'

His hand was up on the trap door again and the little finger hole was just across from him. He moved his hand across to try and push up, but he felt water coming through. Water was coming in through the finger hole. He had pushed the pipe up, but water was still coming in. How could he stop the water? How could he?

'What's up Seoras? What's the matter?' asked Clarissa, and then she burst out laughing again. 'What's the matter? Like something could be worse.'

'Something is worse,' said Macleod. 'The water's coming in through the hole. The pipe's up there, but it's flooding upstairs and it's now coming through the hole down to us.'

'You believe in God, don't you?' said Clarissa.

'Totally,' said Macleod. 'I may not fully understand him, but he watches over me, watches over us all. I don't tell you guys, but I pray every day for each of you. I'm proud of you all.'

'I don't believe,' said Clarissa. 'Too much crap in this world. Too much bad stuff like with these kids. That's the opposite of your side, isn't it? The upside down cross. People actually want to do stuff like this. Why? Why?'

'It's evil,' said Macleod. 'Evil inside of people. They let it stir. We're all capable. All of us, you, me. I just watched a girl get beat by her uncle to get an address.'

'You needed to. You needed to protect these kids.'

'Yes, we justify everything. There's only been one good man,' he said. 'We killed him.'

Clarissa burst out laughing. 'Is that it? Is that your big speech? Is that your big "Let's-convert-Clarissa's speech?"'

'If you don't see a point now, you never will,' said Macleod. 'No, it's not my big conversion speech. I don't do that. Well, certainly not anymore. If you can't see it in me, I'm doing something wrong.

'But we did, didn't we? We did see a point. Things are perfect. These kids are perfect. Then they come into the world and well, they used to say we were born in sin since from the day we were born. I'm not sure I'd go with that anymore, but what I do know is we certainly did our best to screw them up. Screw each other up. Not enough kindness in this world. Not enough humility, not enough . . .'

'Macleods?' said Clarissa, laughing.

'I think we could do with a bit more joy and happiness rather than that,' said Macleod.

Again, she laughed. It warmed him hearing her laugh. If this was to be the last moments, that's what he wanted. He wanted to go out hearing her the way she was, fighting with him, pitching in with the little barbs.

'Looks like you've lucked out,' said Clarissa. 'Looks like He wants you to go and join him.'

'That's what He wants, that's what'll happen. That's the thing. If you believe in omnipotent God, you've got to accept that what He does is what He does. I've given up trying to explain everything. I don't understand it.'

Clarissa's hands touched Macleod's. 'It's been good knowing you,' she said. 'You're a decent man. Wish I could have known you younger.'

'No, you don't,' said Macleod. 'I was miserable then.'

'Miserable then, you're miserable . . .'

The water choked her. She started to cough and shake and fell underneath the water. He dived down to try and lift her up, but she was struggling, choking. This was it. This was the end.

Then light suddenly started to break into the water. A hand in front of his face grabbed Clarissa. Then someone grabbed his shoulders. He was tossed from out of the water into the hallway of the house above. He choked, coughing. Clarissa was rolling over coughing behind him. When he managed to steady himself, Macleod wiped the water from his eyes, tried to focus. He looked up, wondering who his guardian angel was.

Gleary look back at him. 'Bloody hell. You walked into that. You arse.'

Chapter 20

'I never thought I'd be happy to see you, Gleary, but thank you.'

'Just had a feeling,' he said. 'Just had a feeling and I had to know. Don't get this wrong, I'd have happily seen you die in there, but I want my name cleared of all this, and if you went down after coming to see me, that wouldn't happen. Well, let's just say I'm going to go and have a few words with a certain niece of mine, some final words.'

'You don't want to do that,' said Macleod.

'Don't I? You don't cross me, especially not when you're flesh and blood. She done something wrong, fine. If she made a mistake, fine, but you don't cross me. You don't lie to me. Lie to me at a point where I'm going to get pinned on taking out a copper. She set this up. She set it up quick.'

'She's got your smarts,' said Macleod. 'You have to give her that.' He coughed, spitting up a little of the water that he swallowed, while Clarissa fought to get herself upright.

'Well, I'll say thank you,' said Clarissa. 'I thought we were gone there.'

'I take it you have transport up here somewhere,' said Gleary.

'That green sports car,' said Clarissa. 'Did you see it on the way in?'

Gleary turned around to one of his henchmen, who gave a nod. 'You still got your keys on you?'

Clarissa reached down into her pocket and gave a nod.

'Well in that case, I think I'll get off. Don't want to be caught around here. It's not like you two walk out of this and were never down there.'

'You don't have to worry that much,' said Macleod. 'It's not like I can use any of this against you. I came to you because I needed help—because we were the ones that needed help.'

'Yes. Well,' said Gleary, 'the less said about this the better. I'll find out where that package went, don't you worry.'

'I'll come with you,' said Macleod.

'No, you won't. This is family. This is between me and her and you don't get in the way of this one, Macleod. You don't want to see this one.'

Clarissa bent down and helped Macleod up to his feet, as he watched Gleary leave the house. Together the pair of them half stumbled out into the dark night and felt an instant chill across them.

'What now then, Seoras? Does your phone work?'

Macleod pulled it out. 'Looks a bit sodden,' he said.

'I've got a spare mobile in the car,' said Clarissa. 'But I think we should try and get ourselves sorted.'

'It's not like you're going to be able to buy anything tonight. Guess there will hardly be anywhere open.'

'You never know. Supermarkets are open to midnight; some are 24 hours. We'll find something in there. Don't know if it's going to be as good as your hoodie.'

Macleod burst out laughing. 'That's it,' he said. 'That's the one, the little barbs. That's what I would've missed.'

Suddenly he was enveloped from behind, arms flung around his neck. Clarissa hugged him tight. 'I'd have missed a lot more than that,' she said. 'We've done it though. We made it. It wasn't your God either, was it? Gleary—who'd have believed Gleary, a person that wanted you dead?'

'If I say God moves in mysterious ways, you're going to punch me, aren't you?' said Macleod.

'Come on,' said Clarissa. As she started walking her shoes began to squelch. Macleod's did the same.

'Where are we going then?' he asked.

'I say we head back down to Perth. We'll probably find the all-night supermarket, find some clothes in there, get ourselves into one of the cheap hotels, get a shower. I could really do with being looked over. Did we swallow much in there?'

'Can't go to the hospital,' said Macleod. 'Too many questions. We're low-key, remember, I'm not even meant to be in the country.'

'Okay,' said Clarissa, 'but come on, let's get ourselves down to the car. Make sure you dry yourself off as best you can before you get into it. It's real leather on those seats.'

Clarissa and Macleod trudged the short distance back to the little green sports car and once inside it, Clarissa kept the hood up. Windows were rolled up tight and she blasted the heat out through the air conditioning as they trundled their way back to Perth. Slowly, they began to warm up, but Macleod was glad when they found the supermarket. He thought it best if he didn't go in, and Clarissa glared at him. How was she meant to explain this?

'Say you got caught out in a shower,' he said.

'More like a Tsunami.'

She shook her head, asked him again for his sizes before

disappearing inside the store. She came out some fifteen minutes later with several shopping bags, threw them in the boot and the pair drove to the nearest hotel. They picked up a twin room, and Macleod sat down on a chair to let Clarissa go for a shower first. When she came out warmed up, Macleod then revived himself in the shower before changing into the new clothes he'd been given. He sat down on the bed a short time after, coffee in hand, even though it was that rubbish packet stuff.

'I'm kind of hungry,' said Clarissa. 'Let's go out and get something to eat.'

'Okay,' said Macleod, 'but we could also do with getting hold of that phone of yours.'

'You think Hope will still be about?'

'She's bound to be,' he said.

The pair found a fast food burger chain and start eating inside the completely deserted location. Macleod didn't particularly enjoy the Coke that he sucked through the large straw, but there was no way he was having two rubbish coffees on the turn. Once they'd finished, they sat back in the car and Clarissa took out the mobile phone.

'You really want to phone her now?'

Macleod looked at his watch. It had stopped moving.

'What time is it?'

'Well, the car says it's half four.'

'Yes, phone her. She'll probably be awake.'

Clarissa typed in some numbers, then handed the phone to Macleod. He heard ringing at the other end. Then the call was answered, but it took some seconds before someone said something. 'Four-thirty? Got to be something important, John, it's got to be somebody. Hello?'

'Hope,' said Macleod. 'Is that you?'

'Seoras, what's the crisis? What's happening? It's half past four in the morning. I was up until two. I only just got back in.'

'What are you doing out so late?' asked Macleod.

'Kyle Mackie is on the run. We wanted to try and get a DNA swab of off him but he disappeared right through a box in some sort of magic act trick.'

'At least you had the easy evening.'

'Why?' asked Hope. Macleod relayed the events that had led up to their near drowning and he could hear the emotion in Hope's voice when she said she was glad they were all right.

'You and Clarissa, me, this thing's getting too rough, Seoras.'

'Well, I was surprised when Gleary pulled me out, but we need to keep going.'

'Speaking about that,' said Hope, 'I have a new piece of paper. We found it at Kyle Mackie's. It's got symbols on it. I think it's some sort of letter from the group or that. Clarissa had that symbology professor, and I was wondering if we could get it run past her, see if she knows what it means.'

'Send me it,' said Macleod. 'I had to decode one before. Send it to me and I'll see what's it's saying.'

'I'll forward to your phone then.'

'Don't,' said Macleod. 'That's why we're ringing from a different phone. This is Clarissa's spare one from the car.' He pulled it away from his ear and looked at it. 'I think it's a smartphone. It is, isn't it?' He turned and looked at Clarissa who shook her head.

'Yes, it is.'

'Yes, send it to this phone,' he said. 'I'll have a look at it, and I'll get back to you.'

167

'Wait, you okay, Seoras?' asked Hope. 'I mean, really.'

'I don't think now is the time to ask that,' he said. 'Now is the time to just get on with it. Been given a chance, let's make sure we follow it up.'

'But in the meantime,' said Hope, 'I'll send you this and I'm going to catch some shut-eye for a couple of hours. Anything major comes up, just send it through on this.'

'Oh, by the way, Hope,' said Seoras, 'not a word of this to Jane. Not a word of what's happened. She doesn't need that worry. I'll tell her one day when everything's all done, when I'm retired. She doesn't need this sort of thing now.'

Macleod and Clarissa returned back to their hotel room, where Macleod sat on the bed staring at Clarissa's phone and the message that Hope had sent down. He recognised the symbols. He took out of his pocket the damp battered piece of paper that had his decode on it. It took him a while to reconstruct it because the paper was stuck and when he opened it, it ripped, and he lost several letters. Still he sat focused on it while Clarissa was sent off at half past six to seek out a decent coffee. She returned around seven and Macleod was still working at the decode. But by eight o'clock he was holding it in front of him, satisfied.

'I've got it,' he said, 'and you're not going to like it. It says that Kyle is going to atone for his brother. He's going to carry out the next killing. They're all going to start again. They're going to ramp things up because they know we're onto them. There's instructions for a kill going out, but it's over several locations at various pre-stated times. That means the timings come from somewhere else. I can't calculate that. That's from a different message hidden somewhere else.'

Macleod handed his findings to Clarissa, took the phone,

and called Hope back. John answered and she raced from the shower when being instructed that Macleod was on the call.

'What have we got?' Hope asked.

'I've got several locations and I've got a lack of information as well.' Macleod explained what was happening, the content of the message, and the fact the instructions for the next killing would be given out at one of these locations at whatever time.

'I've written them all down, Seoras. I'm going to go and see the DCI. We're going to need to cover this off with manpower, get people everywhere.'

'Absolutely. It's going to be down to a stake out, proper surveillance.'

'I'll submit what I have on paper as well. Not just go to him verbally.'

'We don't have time. Make sure you get them to do this though,' said Macleod. 'You can't cover all these bases together. We'll start to head up that way, but I doubt we're going to get up in time to cover anything off. Let us know what's happening.'

'You don't want to be here either though,' said Hope.

'If somebody's going to killed, I'll be there,' said Macleod. 'Stop the courier, stop the business. I've nearly been killed for this.'

Macleod closed the phone call and told Clarissa they were on the move, but Clarissa produced a couple of croissants. 'You have breakfast first,' she said. 'Then we'll drive up. Take us a few hours, more like three probably but we'll get going. We need to keep it low profile, especially you.'

Macleod pulled on his new hoodie bought the previous night.

'Clarissa, do you think this will still work?' he said. 'Maybe I have to go for the full-on ski mask.'

169

Clarissa shoved him. 'You daft bugger,' she said. 'Get those croissants down, get a coffee, and then let's go. There's not much of a rush anyway,' she said. 'Who knows when the killing's going to actually be?'

'That's exactly why we have to rush,' said Macleod, 'because we don't know. I have a nasty feeling that Hope and Ross are going to be on their own in this one. She's going to need all the backup she can get.'

Chapter 21

Hope phoned Ross, asking to meet him on the way to work and thought about what she could tell the DCI. The man wouldn't be in yet, so she would have to go to his house. She thought about ringing him, but he would just kill the call.

The killings were going to start again; the note in Kyle Mackie's house showed that. But the DCI would ask how they got it decoded. She'd tell him it was a decode done by her source. She could mention the professor but he'd insist on seeing her.

Hope didn't trust the DCI at all. It would be better to have Ross with her, to stop her from losing it because she'd had very little sleep and was liable to snap. She was worried about Macleod and what he'd gone through. She was getting a sick feeling, a nervous tension about the whole matter.

The DCI lived on the edge of Inverness in what some people might have called a modest rich person's house. Truth, he'd probably done well for himself. She saw two BMWs in the drive, parking up, Hope marched in a trademark leather jacket and jeans towards the man's house. She thundered on the door with her fist and Ross pointed out that there was a doorbell.

Hope scowled at him, and he took a step backward as if her wrath was flying toward him.

The door opened on a bleary-eyed DCI Lawson who looked back at Hope. 'This better be good,' he said. 'What time of the day is it?'

'Seven o'clock, sir. Seven in the morning. Most of us are up on the go by now.'

She shouldn't have opened with that. She really shouldn't.

'For what do you need me?' asked Lawson.

'We found something last night.'

'Found something? I thought you lost something. You said you went to get a swab or some sort of DNA sample of Kyle Mackie and he took fright and did a runner. Apparently, he got out from the inside of a house with the two of you there. How the hell did you lose him?'

'Slippery customer, sir, but we found a piece of paper with symbols on it. When we decoded it, we found it's talking about the killing starting up again. There are instructions out there, instructions on how to commit more killings.'

'Symbols and instructions. Who did this decode then?'

'My source.'

'Who is your source? It's time to come clean on it,' said the DCI. 'You need to tell me who the source is.'

'I can't. You'll compromise them.'

'I'm your DCI. We're all here on the same murder team, aren't we? How am I going to compromise him? Come on, behave yourself. Who is it?'

Hope refused. She thought about telling him about the knives' travels, but she couldn't either because of Gleary's involvement.

'We're on the verge of getting something done here. You do

realise that, don't you? We're actually on the verge of getting somewhere. I need some backup to cover several locations.'

'What locations? Where are they?'

Hope produced a piece of paper where she had written down Macleod's locations. The DCI looked them over.

'They are just random bins and places. How did you know where each one of these is? Is there anything about a drop? Drops are usually done at a specific time, so you know when they're there. This could be done any time through the year. You have nothing here. You really don't have anything at all, do you? How do you know these are accurate? Symbols formed into a decode, based on what?'

'Based on other information that has come through other notes.'

'What notes? Where are these notes? Bring these things to me and show me this person that did the decode. I am not doing anything until I speak to them. You'll have me running half the force around over nothing.'

'Nathan Mackie is dead. Kyle Mackie is linked to it. Kyle Mackie was there.'

'If you had a DNA swab, maybe we can prove that, but you cocked that up,' said the DCI. 'I've had enough of this. You can talk to me this afternoon.' The man went to turn away from the door, but Hope put a foot in it.

'You are not walking away from me. You're going to stand here and listen to what I need.'

'Watch yourself, Sergeant.'

'Well, excuse me,' said Hope, 'but did you not hear, these killings will start again?'

'No, they won't. Ian Lamb is dead. Just because some people have had a row, because the Mackies are now falling out with

173

each other, it's got nothing to do with the earlier murders. I told you to investigate Nathan Mackie's death. Now the fact his brother is involved, great, but you screwed up because you lost him. You didn't cover off your bases.'

'You didn't give me the backup,' raged Hope. 'You've dug your head in the sand here time and time again. What is it with you? What the hell's going on?'

'You watch your tone. You just think you can strut around here accusing me of this and that just because you've got some sort of fine figure.'

Hope's eyes flashed anger. She could take anyone commenting on her work but call her a bimbo, and she lit. Hope stepped inside the front door pushing her finger into the chest of Lawson.

'You cocked up. Ian Lamb is dead because of you. You've screwed this up. You've consistently not given me backup. You've consistently not supported my line of attack. You got rid of the one guy who actually got ahead on this.'

'Is Macleod still involved?'

Damn it, thought Hope. *Damn it. Why did I bring him into it?*

'He was on it. You took him off,' she said, rallying. 'You won't even give us spare people. We haven't even got Clarissa on the go at the moment. You didn't step down and take over the DI role, instead you just dumped Ross in it when I was sat in a hospital. I've nearly got killed and . . .'

She stopped. She had nearly blurted out that Macleod and Clarissa had nearly been killed as well.

'What?' asked the DCI.

'You ran Ross ragged with this nonsense. I want to know what your beef is here. Why are you preventing us from going after this? Why are you stopping us from dealing with it?'

Hope could see the man looking around as a few neighbours had come to their doors to see what the commotion was.

'I'd invite you in because this is not tasteful out here,' he said, 'but my wife's asleep and she will not be brought into this. You will come and see me today at two o'clock. We will sit down and discuss what it is that you found. Till then I suggest, Sergeant, that you go home and you get some rest and get yourself into a proper state of mind.'

Cheeky bastard, thought Hope. *A proper state of mind after the lack of effort he's put in, after the lack of backup I've got, after nearly dying.*

Hope turned to walk away and Ross turned with her. She walked slowly clenching her fist because she wanted to turn around and smack the man. She wanted to beat out of him just what he was, incompetent or something else. There was something else there, that kept banging in her head, kept knocking on the door, but she couldn't work it out. She couldn't prove anything.

Slowly, she got into the car, took out the keys, and put them in the ignition. She was aware Ross was watching her.

'What?' she said.

'Is that it?' asked Ross. 'We've achieved nothing. You've marched in there, we've got no backup, nothing. We've got all these addresses to do, and you've achieved nothing.'

'What else was I meant to do?'

This wasn't like Ross. Ross would've kept his council until you asked him. He would never have accused a superior of not managing to do something. If he thought they were lacking, he'd suggest something. He never came on strong.

'I'd suggest you get back to that door and you badger him some more and you make him light up. You make him angry.

You make him fall apart.'

'You think I just fell apart?'

'You did,' said Ross. 'You didn't break down and cry, but you walked away. The boss would be all over him by now. If the boss could move on him, he would. We've had nothing except stonewalling, incompetent management. If he's this bad, how the hell did he get to be a DCI? Tell me that. How did he get to be a DCI? Worked with some rubbish ones but not like this. There's something about this.'

'You feel it too?' asked Hope. 'Are you feeling it as well?'

'Definitely. Something doesn't smell right,' said Ross. 'We've got a countdown running. What are we going to do? Drive around looking? We may have to do it on our own but we could also pull in a few favours. However, if you're sitting stewing and you've got to go back in at two o'clock and talk to this clown. Well then.'

Clown? thought Hope. *He actually used the word clown.* Ross was beyond it. Ross was sold on the idea that DCI is something else. Ross didn't speak like this. This wasn't him. This was him well put out.

Hope gave him a nod, opened the car door, stepped out, slammed the door shut, and she strolled back up the driveway of the DCI's house. She noted that Ross didn't get out. He wasn't going to complain at her. He was showing his trust in her that she would do it. He was also making sure that he wasn't there so that anything that was said between them wouldn't have a second witness.

She approached the door, saw the doorbell that Ross had pointed out previously, and instead smacked the door hard with her fist several times. 'Lawson,' she shouted. 'Get down here you son of a bitch.' Hope continued to bang on the door until it opened, and Lawson's fuming face appeared.

'What in the name of hell is this? I told you I'll see you this afternoon. Get your fancy backside in that car.'

'No,' said Hope. She stood tall over the man looking down at him eyes raging. 'What's your part in all this? What's going on?'

'What the hell do you mean?'

'Nobody is as incompetent as you. Nobody is this bad. Why are you obstructing us?'

'That's a hell of an accusation. You'll lose your career for that one.'

'I don't care,' said Hope. 'It's not about me, it's about kids who have died. What's your part in this? What's going on'

'You will get home and get to bed. When you come in this afternoon if you speak properly to me then I may just keep you on. Remember, I'm the DCI, and I can make you. I can make you a DI. I can get you up to the top but to play with me, you've got to learn to play nice.'

He reached out towards her cheek placing his hand on it. She could see his eyes sweep her body. Hope reached up, took the man's wrist with her left hand, squeezed it tight and bent it, before removing the hand from her cheek.

'I thought Urquhart was his Rottweiler.'

'Don't even start,' said Hope. 'You can stick your cover-up. You can stick it right up your arse. You're responsible for Ian Lamb. He's dead because of you. Macleod was going to take him out. Macleod was going to free him. Macleod understood what was going on and you, you put him out to die. I'll have you, Lawson. You can stick your cover-up and stick it right up your arse.'

'Good,' he said. 'Get out of my house and get out of my

driveway. You've got until the morning to come down on your knees to me and grovel for your job. Otherwise, you're out. Do you hear me? You're out. You won't ever work in this place again, I've had enough of it. I've had enough of you. You're nothing but an overrated piece of totty.'

If it had been an instant reaction she could have been forgiven, but this was a punch that had formed in the back of her mind. Her mind told her not to use her left, instead to swing the hand from below, driving up across the jaw. Lawson came up off one foot and fell back into this hallway. She watched him land, roll over, and then clench his chin. Her fist was sore for she hadn't connected completely correctly, but Hope didn't care. Instead, she stood looking at him and only just for a moment wondered if that was the job gone. She turned, marched back to the car and got in. She started the ignition and began to drive, never looking at Ross.

'I saw nothing,' he said, 'Absolutely nothing.'

'Oh, no,' she said, 'One day you're going to tell them all how I did that.' She looked back at him, her face still furious. 'Stop smiling, Ross,' she said. 'It looks smarmy.'

Chapter 22

'One car each, Alan. You take one site and I'll take the other. Just divide the sites down in the middle.'

'There are about eight sites here,' said Ross. 'We can't cover them all off. No idea when the drop is being made.'

'Well,' said Hope, 'we've just got to make sure we keep going until Seoras and Clarissa get here. They're on their way up. Hopefully, it won't be that long. Have you grouped them? Don't want to be going back and forward on my half when your half is in between. Closest possible route please, Alan.'

She saw Ross stare over at her. 'Of course, you have. Sorry, Alan. Right, let's go.'

Hope took her list, jumped into her car and spotted the first drop site on her paper. Starting up the engine, she drove out of the Inverness police station wrestling the traffic over the Kessock Bridge and down into Kessock. There was a wastepaper bin sitting on a small piece of grass not far from where the local cafe was.

Hope stopped some distance from it, jumped out of the car, throwing her collar up, and walked close up to the bin. She looked inside but could see nothing but a couple of sweet wrappers. She rubbed her hands quickly around it, seeing where you could drop some pieces of paper inside. A few holes in it, but there was nothing there.

Calmly she walked on then came back down the other side of the road keeping an eye on the bin, but there was no one around. *In some ways it was fruitless,* she thought. The drop time could be any time; it might not even be today. They really needed surveillance on all the areas.

Hope jumped back in the car, looked at the next site on the list and routed back across the Kessock Bridge. She looked at the vast expanse of water stretching out along the Moray Firth. She thought she'd have more chance of trying to find a swimmer out there than she would trying to match the timing of her pickup with the drop sites. Ross hadn't phoned, so clearly his first one must have been a bust as well. As she rounded a corner, driving along to where the fire station was, she received a call on her mobile phone.

'We are on our way back,' said the choppy voice of Clarissa. 'Any luck so far?'

'Nothing,' said Hope. 'Absolutely nothing.'

'What'd you get from the DCI?' asked Seoras suddenly.

'Nothing. You better come up with something. I think I've just blown my career,' said Hope.

'Well, that makes two of us,' said Macleod. 'Keep going. There's nothing else for it. So, he gave you no backup whatsoever?'

'I'm out in one car; Ross is out in the other.'

'That's not safe if you find something. It's not safe if somebody is there,' said Macleod.

'I know that Seoras, you think I don't know that? What else do we do? Got to cover the ground. We've got to bust this open. If we don't, the kids are in for it and you and I are down the Swanee.'

'I'm driving as fast as I can,' said Clarissa. 'He's even letting me break the speed limit.'

'Just be careful,' said Hope. 'We'll see you shortly.'

She closed the call, pulled the car up outside on a curb and jumped out, walking past the fire station and down to a small bit of hedge. There was a letterbox, small, ornately shaped, but definitely somewhere you could drop letters into. Hope found this quite strange as there wasn't any house attached to the letter box. It was just sitting on the corner in a hedge. Beyond it was a set of offices.

She walked up, pulled on the letter box and tried to reach her hand inside. When she couldn't, she reached inside her jacket pocket, took out a couple of lock picks and opened up the relatively simple lock in under thirty seconds. There was no letter inside. She fixed everything back again, walked some distance away and sat in the car for a few moments waiting to see if anyone had spotted her who would then come and check. When nobody did, she looked down at the next site on her list.

Over the bridge, she thought. *Over the bridge into the old town.*

Hope manoeuvred the car through Inverness in what was relatively light traffic. If they had been in the later hours of the day, closer to teatime, things would've been really busy. As it was, morning rush hour had just passed for commuters travelling into work, and for this Hope was grateful.

She arrived at a sweet shop, pulled up a little distance from it and then walked back towards it. There was an alleyway down the side of it and she took a left and started feeling her hands down the wall of the sweet shop. There was a brick set aside from the others and there was a small gap in between. She put her hand down but found nothing. Casually, she walked on trying not to look around in case somebody will be following her. That was the other way of getting this done. Somebody spotted them, came to investigate. She could lift them. She could bring them in for questioning. There would be somebody tied into the investigation.

Hope returned to the car and checked the last location on her list. It was on the other side of the river, down near the bank and she drove out of the old town across one of the new bridges, parking up in a side street. Hope got out of the car and marched along the riverfront.

There was a set of railings that ran along preventing anyone from falling down onto the bank of the river. She could see all around her, the daily comings and goings of Inverness, the river being in reasonable flow. As she walked along the railings, she noticed that one of them had the corner piece missing, thereby leaving a standing upright, which was hollow inside. Hope slipped her hand into that hollow and then her heart skipped a beat.

There was paper inside it. Quickly, she slipped the paper up with one hand, put it in her pocket and walked across the street back to her car. Once she sat down inside, she opened up the paper to see it contained a large number of symbols. It was clearly the way they communicated but she didn't know what the symbols meant so she picked up a phone and called Clarissa.

'I'm still coming,' she said. 'It's not been that long since you called us.'

'That's not why I'm calling. I found it. I found the instructions. I'm taking a snapshot of them and then I'm putting them back but if I've got them, that means he won't know where he is going.'

182

'Not necessarily,' said Macleod. 'Could be in any of the other ones. They've probably dropped them in at some point into each one or whatever particular one works at that time of day. You have to guard against drop sites being too hot, so the instructions will be dropped at different ones but at different timings. We may be late in the sequence. You may have got one of the earlier ones. If a murder's not taken place, the person dropping off the details won't know. It's a way of keeping safe.'

'Well, you better get translating this then,' said Hope. 'I'll go back and see if there's anyone about. Call me when you get it translated. Don't be long with it, Seoras.'

'Of course not,' he said. 'Get Ross to you.'

Hope agreed, paused the call, and then made her way back to the riverbank. She filled Ross in on what she was doing on the phone. She told him to meet her and then walked up and down around the drop-off area. As she did so, it became apparent that someone else was walking up and down the other side.

The man was large, six feet four at least, and Hope found that every time she circled, he circled too, and always on the other side of the road. As she walked along, she wondered if she should wait for Ross. The man was big, taller than her, possibly stronger, but she had the element of surprise.

She could get him rather than wait for Ross to turn up because he might scare him off. With the two of them against the man maybe he would consider those to be poor odds and run. As she walked down the river side of the street, she took a glance at him walking up the other side. Another glance told her there were no cars coming along the road at that point and she set off at him without a moment's hesitation.

It took the man a moment to clock that Hope was there and coming at him. When he did, he turned to run. Hope who was now only a few feet from him, flung herself up onto him, her hands going onto his shoulders. She clattered into the back of him causing him to stumble, and trip, and they both fell to the floor. He reached over, first to react, and she had to roll quickly to avoid a fist being planted into her face. She heard the man cry as he punched the ground instead.

Hope got up quickly, clocking the man's face. He stepped forward throwing another punch towards her. She ducked that one, tried to reach up for his arm to drive it up behind his back, but he was strong, very strong, and he turned and threw her back to the ground. As he came down towards her, there were cries on the street, someone shouting to leave that woman alone. He growled at her and turned and ran. A young man, maybe only twenty then stood over Hope offering a hand and asking was she all right.

'I'm fine,' she said. 'Thank you.'

'You should really report this to the police,' he said. 'That's terrible, a broad daylight assault.'

'Detective Sergeant Hope McGrath pursuing a criminal but thank you for your help. It's much appreciated.' The young man smiled, made sure Hope was okay and then she heard Ross arriving.

'Are you okay? What's happened to you?'

'Is this one of your guys,' asked the man. 'Are you okay if I leave you with him?'

'I'm fine,' said Hope. 'This is Detective Constable Alan Ross. He's my partner. Thank you for your help though.' The young man smiled and then took off back along the street.

'Who was it?' asked Ross. 'Did somebody jump you?'

'Big bloke, I'd probably recognise him again, he's got quite the bashed nose. Looks like it'd been broken several times.'

'They'll know we have found the note then,' said Ross.

'They will,' said Hope. 'We'll need to get there quickly in case they call it off.'

The phone rang back. 'Hope, I'm working on it now. I think we're looking for a Janice, Janice Elstree who's got a son by the name of Daniel.'

'Does it have a location though?' asked Hope.

'Working on it,' said Macleod.

Hope turned around to Ross. 'Janice Elstree,' she said. 'Janice Elstree and a child name of Daniel. They didn't get an address but Elstree can't be that…' Hope looked at the man, he was almost in shock.

'The address is flat 2. Flat 2? I think it says Angel's Way. I think it's Angel's Way,' said Macleod over the phone.

'Angel's Walk,' said Ross suddenly. He was listening to the speakerphone on the phone as Macleod spoke.

'Ross says it's Angels Walk not Way.'

'Rathgordon Estate,' said Macleod. 'Does he know it?'

'He seems to but…,' She saw that Ross's face had gone white.

'They're looking to pair us up. They were looking to . . .'

'There's also details on what symbology to write,' said Macleod. 'A lot of it's very similar. Upside-down crosses, numbers now as well. Unholy numbers.'

'Shut up, Seoras. Shut up a minute. Ross,' said Hope. 'What the hell's up? Who's Janice Elstree?'

The man was in complete shock standing there, almost disbelieving what he was hearing.

'What's going on?' asked Macleod over the phone. 'What's going on? I'm going to lose you soon, Hope. It's not easy getting reception down the A9. What's going on? Talk to me.'

'Ross has gone white, sir. I think he knows Janice Elstree.'

'Hope,' said Macleod suddenly. 'Hope, I think I . . .'

The phone line cut off. Hope waited for Macleod to come back on, but there was nothing. She turned back to Ross, 'We've got an address. Let's go. Let's go. Ross?' She grabbed him by the shoulders, shaking him. 'What the hell is it?'

'Janice Elstree, that's the foster mum. Daniel's the child they're going to pair us up with. Daniel's my kid.'

Chapter 23

'We need to move, Ross. Now!'

Hope grabbed the man by the arm, dragging him along the street back to her car. 'Can you drive yours? Are you okay to drive yours?' She looked at him again. Oh no, he wasn't. He was still in shock. 'Snap out of it. Alan, snap out of it. Come on, get in my car. Drive it,' she said.

She handed him the keys and jumped into the passenger seat. Taking out her phone, she dialled the station. 'Requesting backup,' she said to the desk sergeant. 'I need to get police to this address.'

'That's all duly noted,' said the sergeant after Hope had told him the address. 'Just give me a second.'

Hope started waiting on the line as she watched Ross kick back into life. The car sped away towards the Rathgordon estate, but she noticed Ross was on automatic. The paleness was still in the face. The shock was clearly still affecting him.

'Hope,' said the desk sergeant, 'I need to put you on to the DCI. He's down here on the desk talking to me. He needs to have a word with you. He's not happy with this deployment.

'I don't care if he's not happy, just send them. You hear me? Send them.' She knew what she was asking was unfair. If her boss was countermanding this instruction, the desk sergeant wasn't going to be able to enact it.

'I'll put you straight through to him,' said the desk sergeant and before Hope could say anything, she found the line being transferred.

'Sergeant McGrath, what are you doing? Why have I got more people chasing around?'

'I've got a location for the next killing, Sir. I've got a location. Angel's Walk, Rathgordon Estate. I'm on my way with Ross. We need backup. We believe this could be imminent.'

'And what's your evidence for that?'

'I found where they drop the instructions. I have the instructions for the killing.'

'How do you know they're instructions for the killing? You could be on a wild goose chase for all you know. Where did this location come from, this drop location? How did you get it? And anyway, it's about time you came back in. You're running wild out there, I'm not happy with this. I'm going to take over this investigation properly. Get yourself back in.'

'Get me the backup,' said Hope. 'I need the backup now.'

'I'm giving you a direct instruction,' said the DCI. 'Sergeant McGrath, turn that car around, come back into the station, and explain to me everything you've got.'

'I need the backup,' said Hope. 'Now, Lawson, just give me the damn backup.'

'You'll get yourself back in here now or no amount of good looks is going to pull you out of the trouble I'm going to put you in.' Hope swore down the phone and closed the call.

'Damn it, Alan, that arsehole has just turned around and blocked us.'

'He can't. We need this, we need this.'

Hope picked up her phone again as the car raced through the Inverness streets.

'Clarissa, how far out are you? I've got no backup. We're on our own in this one.'

'Then go,' said Macleod. 'We're on our way. We'll meet you at the address.'

'But how far out are you?'

'That'll be twenty minutes. Fifteen if she's pushes the foot down.'

'I always put the bloody foot down,' said Clarissa.

Hope could feel everyone's tension rising. She could feel that everyone had that deep panic about the child and mother who were in trouble.

'See you there. I'll advise if anything changes.'

Hope closed the call as Ross pulled into the Rathgordon Estate. They were some distance from where the first killing had taken place on the other side of the estate. Arriving at the address, they found a small semi-detached house and together ran up to a selection of four doors.

Once again, the building had been split into four separate flats and Hope told Ross to take the two on the right. She took the doors on the left. The first door was green, a hideous shade, something that ran through Hope's mind unwillingly and she banged on it for all what she was worth.

It said flat two. This was the one. This was the one that they would be in. She thumped it again, but nobody responded. Hope spun off to the door beside it, flat one, and banged the door loudly before pressing the doorbell incessantly.

The door opened and a man in his late sixties smiled at her.

'What the hell's up?' he asked. Hope reached inside her jacket and pulled out her warrant card.

'Detective Sergeant Hope McGrath. I need to know where Janice Elstree is and if her child's with her.'

'How the hell should I know?'

'Have you seen her go out this morning? Sorry, this is important.'

'I've just come out of the bath. I've been sat in here the whole time. Heard them about this morning but haven't heard them since. No idea where they are.'

Hope thanked the man and then ran around the side of the house to where Ross was talking to an elderly lady.

'Seems she went out a little while ago. Do you know where they went?'

'She had him in the buggy,' said the woman. 'Usually, they might take a walk up to the golf course.'

'Why the golf course?' asked Ross. 'Is there much of a walk past there.'

Hope knew the course and yes, there were places to walk. There was also a wooded area close to it. More importantly, there was plenty of cover up by the golf course, plenty of hidden places to go.

'I believe he's built a den, the young lad. At least that's what she was telling me. She's good, Janice,' said the woman. 'I mean she does well with all the foster kids.'

'Have you seen anyone else around the house?' asked Hope.

'There was a man earlier on, not long before you arrived,' said the woman.

'What did he look like?' asked Hope.

'He's taller than you, love, and you're really tall for a woman. Don't see many women your height. Lovely red hair with it.'

'The man,' pushed Hope, 'what did the man look like?'

'Got at least four inches on you. Wider, broad? Bit of a

190

smashed-in face.'

Hope's heart sank. That was her attacker. At best, maybe he was coming in to call it off.'

'We need to go,' Hope said. 'We need to go to the golf course, find them quickly.' The pair raced back to the car. 'Have you got a number for her?' asked Hope.

'No, we don't get numbers,' said Ross. 'I just know that's who she is. We've seen Daniel, met him briefly. He's the one they're talking about pairing us up with. Hope, come on.'

'Stop,' said Hope. 'Think. Phone the agency. Tell them it's a police matter. You need her number now.'

'You drive,' said Ross, throwing her the keys and they switched around before Hope sped off towards the golf course. Beside her, she could hear Ross on the phone.

'I'm not trying to interfere,' he said. 'I know it's not normal. We don't tend to . . .'

'Put it on speaker,' said Hope.

Ross placed the phone in front of him, speaker on and Hope heard a rather officious woman on the other end. 'You don't get to speak to those looking after the child except in controlled circumstances.'

'Who am I speaking to?' asked Hope loudly.

'Who else is on the call?'

'This is Detective Sergeant Hope McGrath. I require the phone number of Janice Elstree. I believe she and her child are under threat.'

'What do you mean they're under threat? Why would they be under threat?'

'I believe somebody's after them,' said Hope. 'Detective Sergeant Hope McGrath.'

'I can't just give out numbers like that. You could be anyone.'

'Phone the station, phone the damn station,' said Hope. 'Give them the number. I'll get it from there.'

'There's no need to be like that.'

'I am driving a car trying to prevent the possible murder of this child. Get on with that damn phone number, woman.'

Hope could feel herself losing her cool. Ross picked up the phone.

'You can see this is for real. Phone the station, leave the number. We'll pick it up now. Do it now though, ma'am. Do it right now. Are you going to do it now?'

'I will do it now.'

Ross closed the call. He then dialled the station and waited when they told him that no one had called through yet. It was about three minutes later when they were given the phone number for Janice Elstree.

'Ring it,' said Hope.

'I know,' said Ross. 'Just drive. I'm okay. I've got this bit.'

Hope could see the man's hands were still trembling and they struggled with dialling the number. *Come on, come on, come on, come on,* thought Hope. *Come on. Need our back up too. Where's Macleod and Clarissa when you need them? Where are they?*

'I've got the number,' said Ross. 'Ringing it now.' Hope was bringing the car to a stop alongside the golf club car park.

'Just going to voicemail,' said Ross and then began dictating a message to Janice Elstree to call him immediately.

Hope looked out the window of the car towards the golf course. She thought she could see a very thick-set, tall man.

'That looks like the one with the smashed nose,' said Hope. 'What the heck's he doing there?'

'You don't think he knows where it is or it's going to happen?

Maybe we should go towards him.'

'Well, if he knows where it's happening or he's going there, he's in the middle of the golf course. That woman said about the child's den, building a den. That'll be down by the hedge rows, down along the back, beyond the clubhouse where the train line is.'

Hope got out of the car and ran forward, Ross in tow, but as she did so, she noticed the tall man running across to cut them off.

'You get beyond him. I think he's coming for us.'

Ross ran in front of Hope and the big thick set man ran towards him. He was on an intercept course and would pick him off, but Hope turned from her own course, heading towards the man. Only as she got close did he realise that her intention was not to run past him. Instead, she dropped her shoulder and tackled him, up into the midriff, driving him down to the floor. As she did so, he cradled his arms, encompassing her head, and hit the deck.

He hung onto her as strong as he was before trying to pull her off, grabbing her hair to find the hair tie coming off in his hand. It worked for her because her hair splayed and some of it went straight into his eyes. As he brushed her hair out of the way Hope went to stand up but he grabbed her again by the hair, butting his forehead into hers.

The impact made the world spin. Hope collapsed on top of the man, and he threw her off him. She could see someone in the distance standing up, but she was woozy. She had to react, she had to get going, and she looked at him staring down at her. She drew her foot back and kicked out at his knees, causing him to fall to the ground.

'Oi,' came a shout. Hope didn't know if it was a golfer and

had no idea what was going on but whatever it was, the man bolted. The world was suddenly full of a grey sky and then someone in a Pringle sweater was bent over asking was she all right.

'Are you okay, love. What's he about?' A hand helped her to her feet and four golfers gave her a worried look. Hope didn't wait to thank them but belted off as fast as she could, the world still unsteady around her.

She rounded the clubhouse and heard a cry from below. She looked to her right, saw a steep bank descending down to a railway line, and Ross at the bottom of it.

'Thought I saw something down here,' he said, 'but there's nothing. I don't know where they are.'

'We need to keep going further up. Come on, get back up here. I need you with me just in case we get attacked. Better the two of us together.'

Hope still felt woozy, her head ringing from the butt, yet with each step she felt stronger as if she was more balanced, more focused. She could hear Ross behind her and part of her prayed that Macleod would get here soon. It was just the two of them and with the large man on the scene, who knew who else was here.

'Keep going. Keep going,' said Hope, finding herself out of breath and she watched as Ross took off past her. She was always the fitter one, but Ross seemed almost possessed like nothing else mattered. Then again, this was his child, wasn't it? This was something beyond for him.

'There,' said Ross, 'out there.'

Hope slowed from her run briefly. She stood and looked into the distance. Up ahead, behind a hedge and just about in line of sight, Hope thought she could see someone. She resumed running, pounding across the wet grass as fast as she could. She picked up the phone as she rang.

'This is Clarissa?'

'Golf course beyond the Rathgordon Estate. It's where it's happening. I have no backup. Need you now.'

'Go!' shouted Macleod. 'Go, go. We're on our way. Couple of minutes out. Drive, Clarissa, drive!'

The phone went quiet, and Hope threw it back into her pocket. She kept running, with the occasional stumble, until she arrived at the hedge where they'd seen someone. As Hope arrived behind Ross, they could see along the rear of the hedge, and there was a figure she recognised. Kyle Mackie glared back at them as he had a hand over the mouth of a woman, presumably Janice Elstree.

Chapter 24

'Kyle Mackie,' shouted Hope, partly to see if the man would run, leaving the woman behind. Instead, he looked at her, staring with eyes wide, almost wild. 'Put her down.'

'I've already put her under,' he laughed. 'Already taken her out of the picture. When she wakes up, she'll find a child with markings. A child that . . .'

Ross rushed off from beside Hope. She hadn't instructed him to, he'd simply gone for the man. Hope tried to grab him as he went but missed and ended up following behind him. Ross had a good five or six metres on her, and as he got close to Kyle, Hope saw the man produce a cane and strike with it across Ross's face, sending him tumbling to the ground. Kyle hit him again twice before she got close and he told her to stop, now brandishing an Oriental knife at Janice's throat. She wondered if it was one of the symbol-cutting knives.

'You stay there,' he said, 'or I'll cut her throat.'

Hope looked behind the man and could see a buggy. There was a child asleep inside it. It must have been Daniel. Maybe that's what Ross had seen. For now, Ross was rolling on the floor, writhing in agony. The blow must have been substantial, and Hope edged towards Ross, bending down, putting her hands on him, telling him to stay calm.

'I'm going to leave mum and then I'm going to take the buggy,' said Mackie. 'I have the child.'

'You won't get far. We'll surround you; we'll follow you. There's no way out now, we know who you are as well,' said Hope.

'What does that matter? I'll have done it for him. He'll reward me. Sometimes you have to make sacrifices, but if you sacrifice for him, he'll reward you.'

'Who?' asked Hope. She thought the man sounded like some religious zealot. She'd heard Christians sometimes talk about making sacrifices in this life for rewards later on. Macleod had mentioned it. Of course, he wasn't talking about literal sacrifices, actually killing people, but the parallel was not lost on Hope. 'Who are you sacrificing them for?'

'Can't you tell? Didn't we tell you? Your boss knows. We're in the shadows. We're not in your face like they are, but with each one, what we do builds, and we'll offer him a real sacrifice soon enough, a true one, and the blood of the children will run. The blood of the children will set us free to do what we want, will set him free.'

When the man said the blood of the children, Hope shivered but she was always also intrigued. To set them free. Set him free. They were talking like some sort of cultists. What was it they hoped to achieve?

She was struggling. She usually understood other murderers. They did it for cash. They did it because of some sort of slight. There was always a reason, and though she never thought any reason good enough to murder someone, there was some sort of logic, some sort of explanation to fall back on. She'd once talked with Macleod about whether people were evil, and he always said no, not completely. Some were misguided, some were overcome with greed or revenge, but they weren't truly evil. She found herself doubting that statement now.

Hope watched as Kyle Mackie kept the knife at the woman's throat as he dragged her backwards towards the buggy. Hope helped Ross to his feet but the man was groggy. She could see blood running from the side of his mouth, a massive bruise forming on the side of his face, but she had to hang onto him. He was almost ready to collapse again.

Kyle Mackie dropped the blade from the woman's throat and quickly turned to the buggy. He lifted the child out, held it close with a knife above it. 'Any closer, I'll kill him.'

'Daniel,' yelled Ross, 'Daniel.' She could see Ross trembling and wondered just how in control of his actions he was.

'There's no way out,' said Hope, to which Mackie laughed.

'Why not, aye? I'll just make off with the child. There's only you and him, and look at him. The man's a mess. He'll get the treatment again if he comes near me. You should really get stronger people around you, Detective Sergeant. You need people to guide you properly, but you don't accept guidance, do you? We're everywhere. That's the thing, we are everywhere.

'You should stand with us because we don't tolerate failure. It makes you stronger, makes you capable. I never thought I could carve into the back of one like this, but they showed me. You learn what you can do, what you can be, but it doesn't matter. There'll be another one. All these single mums, children without fathers, what does it say? Look after the orphans and the widows? Stuff that. Slash them, kill them, use them, but there'll be plenty more.'

In the background, Hope could hear a commotion and then

she heard a car. She saw Mackie staring over her shoulder into the distance through the hedge. Hope quickly flicked her head around to see what was happening.

Although the view was fairly masked, she saw a car driving along one of the golf holes, several irate golfers shouting, and a woman in the front seat. There was an older man beside her. At least she thought the frame looked older, but he was wearing a hoodie so she couldn't see his face. Hope didn't stare for long, instead, flicking her head back to look at Mackie. She could sense that his monologue was faltering, now beginning to panic.

'We've got you covered. You'll go down for this one,' said Hope.

'Like hell,' said Mackie. 'It doesn't matter how you kill them, does it?'

He flung Daniel off to one side, so the child tumbled down the large bank towards a railway line at the bottom. Mackie turned on his heel and began to run away and Hope stepped over to the bank looking down. The child was on the railway line, and in the distance, a sound shook Hope to the core. There was a train coming.

'Daniel,' shouted Ross, and bolted immediately onto the slope and began to tumble. Hope saw the man descend and saw Mackie running. Her case, her career was disappearing on one side, a child's life was in the balance on the other.

'You've got him, Alan, you've got him.' Hope turned and ran for Mackie.

* * *

Alan Ross tumbled, his head still woozy, before he felt the

199

wooden sleeper banging into his back. As he tried to stand up, he found everything was groggy and he looked across at the child now lying on the railway lines. The vibration was there from the train, the vibration, something telling him it was coming. He couldn't stop the train. But it wasn't in view yet. Maybe he could get there.

Ross got up onto his knees, tried for his feet but struggled, and then shuffled forward on his knees, collapsing beside the child. The child was now crying from the fall, wailing at the top of its voice, and Ross reached out with a comforting hand.

'I've got you, Daniel,' he said, 'I've got you.' He struggled to get to his knees again but pulled the child into him. 'We need to get you off these tracks. We need to get you.'

Ross's head swam. It was like the trees were moving. It was like everything was going in circles. He tried to grab a breath, tried to focus. He looked to his right. There was a train and then a siren. The loud diesel horn blaring. Daniel didn't like it. The child screamed more. Ross tried to react, but he wasn't sure which direction he was walking. Were they going towards the train? Were they going . . .

'My bloody foot,' shouted someone, 'my bloody foot.'

Ross was aware someone was standing beside him as arms went around his shoulders. He stumbled backwards as he was pushed, and then he collapsed onto wet grass as a rush of wind went past him. Daniel was in his arms as thundering carriages continued past. It was like they would never stop, like they would never end, and then they were gone.

Ross tried to sit up, but he couldn't. He looked to his left and saw the face of an older woman. Purple hair. She was breathless.

'I got you, Als, and we got this one.'

Ross didn't know what was happening, but in his arms was a young boy no more than a couple of years old.

'This is Daniel,' he said. 'This is Daniel.' Tears streak down his face. 'This is my Daniel.'

* * *

Hope McGrath jumped through the hedge, aware that a car was coming up behind her. It wasn't far off and she wondered how long it would be before it caught up with her. Ahead of her, she saw Mackie cut through behind some trees. He wasn't that far away. If she could just keep going.

She was clearly the superior athlete, clearly had a longer stride and was quicker despite the wooziness she felt. She sprinted between the tree and the hedge, rounded the corner and then felt something hit her in the head. It was probably the cane, the stick he'd beaten Ross with. The bastard had waited for her.

She took the first blow in the head, stumbled backwards into a tree, but managed to duck as the cane then hit the tree. Hope stood swaying but put her arms out and took the blow of the next strike of the cane on her arms. She yelled, cursed, but when he went to swing again, she grabbed his wrist, twisting it hard.

The cane dropped and she drove a knee up into his stomach. She heard the 'oof' and then grabbed him and threw him against a tree. The man's head smacked off it. He fell down in front of her.

'I've got him,' she yelled. 'I've got him. Seoras, I've bloody got him.'

Hope felt somebody grab her head. She was hauled by the

hair, her forehead smacking off the tree, and she fell to the ground. Something went into her arm, a stabbing pain racing up it. She cried out in agony, but somebody put a foot on her chest.

'Just finish the bastard,' said a hard voice.

She looked up and saw the smashed nose, the tall man. As her head rolled to the side, she saw Mackie being held head up, his neck exposed and a knife whipped across it. Blood poured out and they let the man drop. The foot on her was driven into her stomach and she doubled up, feeling like she was going to vomit. There was a car horn, a cry from somebody telling him to go, then the man was away. All of them were away.

Maybe ten seconds later, someone knelt down beside her, took her by the arms, holding her tight. She cried out for the knife that'd been stuck in her arm. The wound was suddenly clasped by this person.

'My arm,' she said, 'My bloody arm.'

'Got you. I've got you.'

'Seoras, Seoras, they're away. They're gone.'

'But I've got you. I've got you. You're okay. You're okay.'

He helped her up to a sitting position before he began to build a tourniquet on her arm, ripping off strips of his clothing to do it. She heard phone buttons being pressed and then he said, 'This is Detective Inspector Seoras Macleod. I have wounded colleagues. Location is…' He told them the golf club. He told them where.

'You can't be here,' she said in a woozy fashion. 'We've lost them. We've lost our trail.'

'Quiet,' said Seoras. 'Quiet. We'll get them. We'll get them, but I need you in a hospital.' She leaned forward into his embrace and let Macleod hold her tight. She hoped they got the child. She prayed Ross had got the child.

Chapter 25

'Seoras, it's good to see you; you don't look too bad considering.' The Assistant Chief Constable held his hand out to Macleod who shook it gladly.

'Thanks for everything you did with Jane, kept her out of most of this. Don't talk to her about what else has happened.'

'You seem to have got somewhere with the case; how did things go?'

'I won't lie to you we did some investigation on our own, dug up a few trails.'

'I really don't care,' said Jim, 'but please sit down.' The rather posh hotel on the outskirts of Inverness was a good setting. Macleod was looking forward to this evening, for Jane was returning home. Clarissa was going to pick her up and drive her as Macleod had got called to a meeting with the Assistant Chief Constable.

Jim was being called in to troubleshoot what had happened. Macleod knew he was well aware that the force had got lucky for the DCI had publicly decried Macleod who had said there was another killing coming. They had turned around and blamed it all on Ian Lamb and investigations would continue into that.

They'd also not listened to either Hope or Ross, the DCI, seemingly not wanting to follow up their leads. Now Jim would have to come in and clean up. Macleod was fully expecting to be asked to do the investigative side, but how things would look from above and from the public's point of view would need to be taken care of by somebody at a much higher level. That was going to be Jim's role.

'I was going to ask if you want coffee, but I ordered it anyway.'

'Is it proper coffee?' asked Macleod.

'I don't really have the same obsession,' said Jim. 'I ordered coffee, black, is that okay?'

It wasn't but Macleod wasn't going to let on, so he simply nodded and then watched cautiously as two cups arrived along with a flask of coffee. Jim poured Macleod one and then himself, before he sat down with his legs crossed looking slightly beyond Macleod.

'It's been a right glorious cockup, hasn't it? What do you make of him?'

'What do I make of who?' asked Macleod.

'The DCI. Did he do it deliberately or has he done it because he simply doesn't like others being in the limelight?'

'From what Hope told me,' said Macleod, 'he doesn't seem to want to take charge either, at one point leaving Ross running an entire investigation. Ross is very capable but that's not for him. Lawson should have stepped in on that one. He jumped to conclusions over me, quick to hand me to the wolves, and he humiliated me in front of all the press.'

'Well, I'll put that right,' said Jim. 'I'll reinstate you to the case publicly. You'll be with me, and I'll make it quite clear that you were in the right all along. I think it's the least I can do, to say we're investigating.'

'No,' said Macleod. 'Make your statement if you wish, do it quietly. We don't need a lot of excitement around this. Also, don't jump too quickly on the DCI.'

'Why not? He absolutely went through you; he hung you out to dry, Seoras. Man deserves what's coming to him.'

'Maybe, but I don't do vengeance and what I'm certainly not going to do is have this all be about what the force did. I need my officers focused on what's ahead. I need them looking for where the next murder is. I need them sorting out what's going to happen. Can't have a circus running at the same time. There's also the idea that if the DCI is not just incompetent, not just an egotist, it may be better to have him unawares.'

Jim sat back, the big man taking his coffee to his lips. He took a good gulp before putting the cup back down. Macleod could see him thinking.

'You really think that's what it is? You think he's really gone that way?'

'I don't know,' said Macleod, 'I need to investigate. We start by going deep into the lives of the Mackie brothers. They were heavily involved in this. I believe that Nathan Mackie killed the second child, his niece, and then his brother killed him because he screwed it up so badly,' said Macleod. 'I mean he went to bed with his sister, his twin, that's why the DNA was so similar. There's some sort of group here. I said it earlier on, I didn't think the killings were all done by one person, they were all so similar yet subtly different.'

'You think it's like a cult, a club?'

'Very much. The symbols could be a smoke screen. Clarissa saw them all meeting and what worries me is these people are not your standard criminal. They're all people who've not done things before. That's going to make them very hard to catch. I'm not quite sure where we go from here other than get into the Mackie brothers' lives, find out who they were with. I'll get Clarissa to draw a mock-up of those people she saw, get it out to the public, see if we can find anyone. Forensics are coming up with very little. We'll need to improve on that.'

'Do you think they'll strike again?'

'With what was said to Hope by Mackie, there's something coming, big, bigger than what we've had so far.'

Jim looked very dour. 'Well, God help us then, Seoras, because this has been brutal. Kids. I mean, kids.'

'I know,' Macleod said, 'the team struggled with it as well.'

'Then I'll play it your way; you get straight back onto it tomorrow morning; bring your team together. How is Hope doing anyway?'

'Lucky enough with the knife wound. It wasn't a deep cut, it didn't go in that far, so she'll heal. She'll not be operating in full capacity with it for a while though, but she wants to come back in. Ross, well, he took it hard, but at least he's okay. He's got a bit of bruising around the face but no permanent damage. Clarissa got to the pair of them—saved both him and the child.'

'It was the child he was going to adopt, wasn't it?' said Jim. 'Is that true?'

'Completely true, though that doesn't go public. We'll regroup in the morning. I'll pull them in, and we will get on this, but it's not going to be pretty,' said Macleod. 'These people are fanatical, and worse than that, they're quietly fanatical. They're not the people charging around in front of you to make an image for themselves. I believe they actually are on board with whatever it is they're doing, whatever sort of worship they think they're at. These are ritual killings.'

207

'God help us,' said Jim. 'We'll get whatever resources we can behind you. Just get me these people.'

Macleod stood up, drank the rest of his coffee, and shook Jim's hand. 'I'd stay and talk, Jim, but Jane's just got home, and I had to leave her in the company of Clarissa for the evening. I might get to spend my one evening before I'm back into the maelstrom.'

'Of course. I'm on the phone if you need me. I'll brief you about what I'm going to do with the press and how I do it. You don't go near them. If there's public briefings to be done, we need to show that higher up are taking a deeper interest anyway for the public's sake.'

'Good,' said Macleod. 'I'll work it out. Trust me, I'll work it out. I just hope I can get to it before the worst happens.'

Macleod turned away, walked to the front door of the hotel and hailed a taxi. He sat in the back and murmured when the taxi driver asked him was he that detective off the telly. Macleod said he never watched Columbo so he wouldn't know. The driver gave a little laugh before looking back at the road and taking his cue to be quiet.

The rain was pouring down. When Macleod stepped out of the taxi and walked to the front door of his house, the little green sports car was parked in the drive, and the door opened as he was halfway down.

'Seoras!' He looked up and saw Jane running down the driveway and she flung her arms around him, almost knocking him over.

'Easy, woman,' he said. 'I was glad you didn't jump. I wouldn't have been able to catch you.'

'Are you okay?' she said, 'They said that . . .'

'We're all okay. We're all okay. Few bumps and bruises, but

we're fine. I hope Clarissa hasn't scared you with what's been happening.'

'Seen it in the papers, heard too much, but at least, nothing happened when you two were investigating.'

Macleod smiled. Clarissa appeared at the door and he took Jane's hand, walking her back to the house. As they reached the door, the woman with purple hair stood blocking their entrance.

'I guess you just kicked me out then. You two youngins will want to be left alone.'

'Is he like that in work?' laughed Jane. 'I haven't seen that side of him.'

Macleod gave her a dig and said, 'It's best not to look embarrassed,' as he squeezed past Clarissa.

'Oh, there's an envelope for you,' said Jane. 'In the kitchen, I've left it there.'

Macleod walked through and Clarissa followed him. When Jane entered the kitchen, Macleod turned to her.

'Would you give us a moment, love? I need to clear up some stuff around the case. It's not pretty. Probably best if you're not here and then I'm yours for the night.'

'The excitement never ends,' said Jane. 'I'm thinking of running a bath.'

'What's he going to do?' asked Clarissa.

'It's for him,' said Jane. 'Likes his back scrubbed.' She gave a cheeky wink and left the room. Macleod smiled, but it quickly fell.

'What's the matter?' asked Clarissa.

'The envelope. Look at it. Typed, and the stamps. Old stamps. Not bought recently. Made sure we're not going to be able to trace this one,' he said.

She looked at him quizzically. He grabbed the letter opener from the side of the kitchen, cut through the top of the envelope, and took out a white piece of paper. He opened it up and there were cut-out letters from magazines and newspapers. It had an address on it. Nothing else, just an address in the random cut-outs

'Who's sending you that?' asked Clarissa.

'Gleary,' said Macleod. 'Gleary said he'd get me that address. Last thing he said to us.'

'He did, didn't he? So, he must have gone back and got the address from her. That's a stroke of luck, isn't it? Somewhere else to go.' Macleod turned away and she tapped him on the shoulder. 'What? What's the matter? It's good news this, isn't it?'

He picked up the phone and dialled a number for Glasgow Police Station, the main one in the centre of town. He asked for a Detective Sergeant Smith and was put through.

'Andy, this is Seoras.'

'How are you doing? Been hearing about the stuff up north. Doesn't look good.'

'Well, I'm back on the case,' he said. 'Meantime, have you had any unusual deaths in your area?'

'What do you mean?'

'Gang lords, dealers, people who are running drugs?'

'Hang on a minute.' Macleod heard him type into the computer. 'Female found at the top of a block of flats. Oh,' he said 'Not pretty. Not pretty at all. I mean, they found her in several bits around the flat. Oh, blimey. It's not one you want to get called out to. Why? You got an interest in it?'

'No,' said Macleod. 'It's not what I'm looking for. Forget I called.'

He put the phone down, looked up at Clarissa who read his face.

'What'd he do?'

'He made a statement. She was in different parts of the apartment when they found her.'

'Are you okay? You know who was involved. She's not innocent of anything.'

'No, but neither are we. We pushed it, we . . .'

'She tried to kill us, Seoras. She tried to kill you and she tried to kill me. Trust me. I'm not having a problem dealing with this.'

'Go and get some sleep,' he said. 'Go and get some sleep.'

'Are you going to be okay?' she asked.

Macleod turned, gave her a smile. 'There's a woman in there that needs my attention tonight and she'll get the smiling, happy-go-lucky man that she thought she might have moved in with, but trust me, at this point in time, I wish I did drink because I want to forget what I've just heard.'

'Tomorrow morning then,' said Clarissa. She stepped forward, put an arm on his shoulder, and kissed his forehead. 'She's a lucky woman.'

Macleod held the letter as Clarissa left and then he took a piece of paper and wrote down the address. He crumpled the original letter and envelope up into his fist and walked through to his living room.

'I have the fire going,' said Jane.

'Good,' said Macleod. He tossed the envelope and letter in his hand into the burning fire.

Read on to discover the Patrick Smythe series!

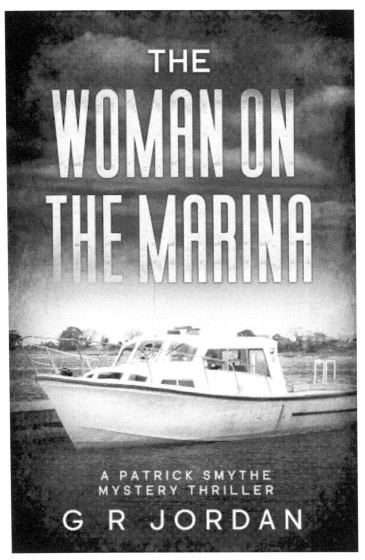

THE
WOMAN ON
THE MARINA

A PATRICK SMYTHE
MYSTERY THRILLER

G R JORDAN

Start your Patrick Smythe journey here!

Patrick Smythe is a former Northern Irish policeman who

after suffering an amputation after a bomb blast, takes to the sea between the west coast of Scotland and his homeland to ply his trade as a private investigator. Join Paddy as he tries to work to his own ethics while knowing how to bend the rules he once enforced. Working from his beloved motorboat 'Craigantlet', Paddy decides to rescue a drug mule in this short story from the pen of G R Jordan.

Join G R Jordan's monthly newsletter about forthcoming releases and special writings for his tribe of avid readers and then receive your free Patrick Smythe short story.

Go to https://bit.ly/PatrickSmythe for your Patrick Smythe journey to start!

About the Author

GR Jordan is a self-published author who finally decided at forty that in order to have an enjoyable lifestyle, his creative beast within would have to be unleashed. His books mirror that conflict in life where acts of decency contend with self-promotion, goodness stares in horror at evil, and kindness blindsides us when we at our worst. Corrupting our world with his parade of wondrous and horrific characters, he highlights everyday tensions with fresh eyes whilst taking his methodical, intelligent mainstays on a roller-coaster ride of dilemmas, all the while suffering the banter of their provocative sidekicks.

A graduate of Loughborough University where he masqueraded as a chemical engineer but ultimately played American football, Gary had worked at changing the shape of cereal flakes and pulled a pallet truck for a living. Watching vegetables freeze at -40'C was another career highlight and he was also one of the Scottish Highlands "blind" air traffic controllers.

These days he has graduated to answering a telephone to people in trouble before telephoning other people to sort it out.

Having flirted with most places in the UK, he is now based in the Isle of Lewis in Scotland where his free time is spent between raising a young family with his wife, writing, figuring out how to work a loom and caring for a small flock of chickens. Luckily, his writing is influenced by his varied work and life experience as the chickens have not been the poetical inspiration he had hoped for!

You can connect with me on:
- https://grjordan.com
- https://facebook.com/carpetlessleprechaun

Subscribe to my newsletter:
- https://bit.ly/PatrickSmythe

Also by G R Jordan

G R Jordan writes across multiple genres including crime, dark and action adventure fantasy, feel good fantasy, mystery thriller and horror fantasy. Below is a selection of his work. Whilst all books are available across online stores, signed copies are available at his personal shop.

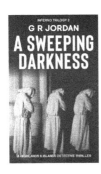

A Sweeping Darkness - Inferno Book 3
https://grjordan.com/product/a-sweeping-darkness
The public weeps as the killings begin again. With the chase now on, agendas are quickly accelerated. Can Macleod and McGrath pull together a ragged investigation to stop an unholy sacrifice?

Reinstated but still under the public glare, DI Macleod knows that the dark cult responsible for the first deaths are now feeling the pressure. Tales of brutality and sacrifice run rife leaving Macleod to sort rumour from reality. As the true nature of what the cult intends to do comes to light, Seoras and Hope find themselves in a desperate race to find missing children and Ross's adopted child.

For the love of God, he has to find them!

A Personal Favour (A Kirsten Stewart Thriller #9)

https://grjordan.com/product/a-personal

A friend's daughter goes missing when reporting for a local paper. A town on the up but with a history steeped in blood. Can Kirsten break the steely cocoon of silence and find the girl before she is another tragic story?

Dealing with the desperate change in their circumstances, Craig receives a plea from an old friend to find his missing daughter. Being in no shape to assist, Kirsten takes his place and finds herself in a cold wilderness that lacks a warm welcome. When she digs too deep into the past, a desperate town seals itself off, leaving Kirsten trapped within.

Some stories are just too personal for the public to hear!

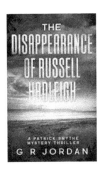

The Disappearance of Russell Hadleigh (Patrick Smythe Book 1)
https://grjordan.com/product/the-disappearance-of-russell-hadleigh
A retired judge fails to meet his golf partner. His wife calls for help while running a fantasy play ring. When Russians start co-opting into a fairly-traded clothing brand, can Paddy untangle the strands before the bodies start littering the golf course?

In his first full novel, Patrick Smythe, the single-armed former policeman, must infiltrate the golfing social scene to discover the fate of his client's husband. Assisted by a young starlet of the greens, Paddy tries to understand just who bears a grudge and who likes to play in the rough, culminating in a high stakes showdown where lives are hanging by the reaction of a moment. If you love pacey action, suspicious motives and devious characters, then Paddy Smythe operates amongst your kind of people.

Love is a matter of taste but money always demands more of its suitor.

Milton Keynes UK
Ingram Content Group UK Ltd.
UKHW041257230724
1000UKWH00009B/13

9 781915 562234